Limit Bid! Limit Bid!

Charles Baxter Clement

Jameson Books
Ottawa, Illinois

To Foots and Catharine

1

H E HAD NEVER seen anything like it before. There must have been over a hundred guests, each decked out in fancy, warm-weather hunting gear. Then there were the black servants—at least fifty—all dressed in white coats and uniforms, the men wearing tidy black bow ties. But it was the house and grounds which awed him: a big, two-storied, used-brick mansion set in the middle of a grove of great red oaks, its two wings reaching out and back to surround a graceful swimming pool. Never had he been so close to such wealth and style.

The drive down from Memphis into the Mississippi Delta had presented a fitting prelude. The September morning sky was pale blue and cloudless, seemingly having lifted itself higher, taking with it the heat and dust and humidity of summer. The flat, fertile fields stretching into the distance were far different from the lonely, misty valleys of east Tennessee. They were much like all his new life farther west: open and limitless.

Richard would have been much more self-conscious if he had known the quiet attention he was receiving. He was over six feet tall with a shock of thick blond hair. His pale gray eyes and slender, athletic posture made him appear almost Prussian. And Delta women had an eye for handsome young men, just as they did for fine horseflesh and prize breeding cattle. But it was the nature of the invitation which made him most uncomfortable. He had never met Warwick Morgan and was confused when he was invited to his exclusive dove hunt.

Being a stranger, he stationed himself next to one of the huge oaks and watched the busy preparations. A long bar next to the pool was doing brisk business with the hunters. On the other side was a crew of young men setting up musical equipment and a wooden dance floor. Beneath the trees was another group arranging row after row of covered tables and chairs. Beyond them stood a line of mule-drawn flatbed wagons, their fieldhand drivers talking animatedly in a circle. It was a scene more from the 1850s than from the early 1970s.

Richard looked down at his Sears hunting clothes and the old twelve-gauge his father left him when he died. It was a Parker, one of the finest guns made in its day. His father had worked over three weeks rebuilding a barn for a local banker in exchange for it. It still shot as well as the day it was made. Richard had had lots of practice at Harvard in meeting new, sophisticated people, but it was still painful to be surrounded by such opulence. He simply reminded himself—as his family had always done—that it was the person, not the clothes, that counted. It was then that he looked up and confronted the prettiest girl he could ever remember seeing.

She was about five-eight, with long, straight, dark auburn hair. Her skin was fair and blemishless, except for

2

tiny hints of rose-colored freckles. Her nose was straight and perfectly proportioned, except for a barely perceptible bump at the bridge, as if she had fallen as a little girl. But the crowning feature was her smile. A natural reticence seemed to war in the musculature of her face with what must have been a truly generous nature. It was difficult to watch her struggle without grinning.

"Hello," she said in a soft, southern voice much lower than one would have expected. "I'm Irene Moody. You must be the lawyer War talked about."

Richard finally realized he was grinning broadly and sputtered, "Yes, yes, I'm Richard Johnson—nice to meet you."

They faced each other for several seconds, until Irene said, "I can tell from your voice that you're not from around here."

"Oh, I'm from near Johnson City—east Tennessee," he blurted, suddenly afraid that would little interest her. "I guess I'm a hillbilly."

She obviously liked the answer. Her smile was radiant, as she said, "Well, hillbillies drink Bloody Marys, don't they? War's father invented the fresh-juice variety. Let's see if they have any left."

They walked toward the lively crowd of hunters mingling near the bar. It disturbed Richard that everyone was drinking before a dove hunt, but he was fascinated with their poise and animation. Everyone seemed to know everyone else, someone constantly interrupting another conversation to ask about business or a member of the family. It was comforting to be around such familiarity, so different from the formal distances practiced at home.

Irene ordered two drinks and turned to ask, "Where do you practice—downtown?"

"Yes," Richard replied. "I'm with Heiner, Player, and Ide. I do mostly corporate work."

"War said that," she said, sipping her drink through a straw. "He said you were some kind of international *expert*."

"Oh, heck, an expert's someone from out of town," Richard sputtered. "They hired me to do that kind of work, but I'm far from an expert."

Richard was having trouble concentrating. While walking to the bar, he had had the opportunity to look the girl over. She was virtually his ideal: long legs, slender waist, generous bosom. She was dressed in a printed cotton frock, the simplicity of which framed the beauty of her features. "Are...are you Warwick's...girlfriend?" he asked, dreading the answer, for how could he compete with such grand trappings?

A look of surprise came to Irene's face. But before she could answer, a wagon driver began beating an enormous steel triangle, signaling the hunters to board the wagons. The crowd responded and began drifting off the terrace.

"I'm not going to shoot," Irene said, her smile having vanished. "I'm going to stay here. You're supposed to ride with War on the last wagon—just wait for him there."

The two stared at each other for what seemed a second

too long. Then a faint smile crossed her lips, and she turned to walk toward the house.

"I hope to see you after the hunt," Richard said, not knowing if he was heard above the din of the party. Apparently he wasn't, as she continued walking and vanished quickly through a screen door.

Richard turned slowly, confused as to direction. He hadn't met a girl like Irene since moving to Memphis and was beginning to feel his loneliness. Memories of previous liaisons flickered through his mind like old injuries aggravated by the weather. He found himself staring at the swimming pool.

But then he sighed and turned toward the wagons. Half of them were full, and the others were surrounded by the chattering crowd. One was parked off to the side. He picked up his shotgun and strolled forward. Once again he felt overwhelmed by the ease and familiarity with which the others faced such luxury. When he reached the wagon, he started to sit down, but a large, black driver said, "'Scuse me, suh, but thas Mista' Warwick's wagon."

Richard paused for a moment and then said, "I'm supposed to hunt with him."

"Oh, fine," the driver answered. "Heah, let me have yo' shotgun."

The man took the firearm, and Richard relaxed. It was cool under the trees, but he could tell the day was heating up, with great shafts of light slanting through the trees onto the soft grass. He sat for a number of minutes watching all the others leave, and then he and the driver were alone—even the bartenders and table crews had left. Then he heard the sound of footsteps and looked up to see a tall, slender, dark-haired young man of about his own age striding up the road from the barns.

He had almost Italianate features: clear, light caramel skin, a large, straight nose. His eyes were big and coal black. He wore a light khaki hunting vest over a white cotton dress shirt and seersucker trousers. His glossy black hair bounced as he walked.

"Get 'er rollin', James," he commanded, leaping onto the flatbed. "I wanna' go way to the end of the ol' Smithson place."

"Yassuh," the driver answered gleefully, slapping the reins against the backs of his mules.

The wagon lurched and began lumbering down the rutted road toward the fields. For several minutes Warwick said nothing, but simply leaned against the front board of the wagon, staring straight ahead. Richard felt both awkward and annoyed. Was Morgan being rude to him? Why had he been invited? Finally, he stood and, balancing himself, walked toward the front.

"I'm Richard Johnson," he announced, holding on with one hand and extending the other.

"Yeah, I know," Warwick replied, his eyes continuing to search the road ahead. "Whatcha bring to kill birds with?"

"Uh, a twelve-gauge," Richard replied, looking about swiftly, until he remembered the driver had taken it.

"That'll do," Warwick said, his eyes still glued ahead. "If you want some shells, James' got 'em."

"Thanks," Richard replied, wondering how long this awkward relationship would continue. Then slowly Warwick turned toward him, his eyes focusing on Richard's. And it was as if he had a disability, as if he could only concentrate on one object at a time: first the eyes, then the nose, the mouth, the clothes, taking in some very important critical information, in a process which appeared almost painful. After a few seconds, he turned away again.

The two rode in silence, as the wagon slowly left the protection of the trees and made its way through fields of cotton plantation. The dirt in the road was cocoa brown and powdery, the mules creating quiet, controlled explosions with each step. The day was perfectly still, and the only sounds were the muffled movements of the animals and the constant clicking of harness.

Warwick remained frozen, but just as one would have given up hope, he leaped from the wagon and ran into a row of cotton plants. He stripped a branch from one of the bushes and trotted back.

"Here," he said, jumping aboard and tearing away the foliage. "Ever seen cotton? This triangular thing is the flower. For some goddamn reason, they call it a 'square.' When it matures in a couple of weeks," he continued, ripping open the light green pod, "this stringy, sticky mess becomes cotton fibers—the stuff they weave into T-shirts and sheets."

"It sounds pretty simple," Richard said, remembering

the painstaking effort and backbreaking work required to grow even a small patch of tobacco on his parents' farm.

"Well, it ain't," Warwick muttered, wiping his hands in the straw on the bed of the wagon. "You have to be a goddamn scientist to grow the stuff—and a graduate economist. Soil tests, hybrids, fertilizers, pesticides, insecticides, interest rates, machinery—hell, they've taken all the nature out of the business. That's why I keep a few blacks around the place—they were the human part of farming when I was a boy."

The wagon came to a stop underneath a weathered oak standing in the middle of a harvested cornfield. The driver jumped down and began unloading the equipment, including a camp table and a camouflaged cooler for drinks and lunch. Warwick unloaded two canvas chairs and placed them next to the table, facing the field. The driver climbed back aboard his wagon, whipped his reins, and started toward the house.

"Wanna beer?" Warwick asked, bending over the cooler.

"Sure," Richard replied, laying his shotgun on the table and stretching.

"They could start flying any minute now," Warwick mumbled, fumbling with the metal top to a can. "They ought to be coming from straight in front of us. There's a lot of corn left in this field, and I haven't let anyone shoot it yet. When they start comin'—and it could be anytime—I'll stand over there to the right and you to the left. Let me fire first, then you shoot whenever you want. I like to let 'em get in real close on the first pass. It's like they learn to trust the field, regardless how many get shot."

Richard nodded and sat down to enjoy the beer, while Warwick busied himself arranging shotguns and ammunition on the table. Richard noticed how intensely he concentrated on his task, how deftly he moved—he might have been a surgeon performing an operation. Once finished, Warwick returned to the cooler and produced sandwiches and fried chicken. They ate in silence.

"Is this what you do?" Richard asked, while munching on a drumstick. "You a farmer?"

"Oh, yeah," Warwick answered very slowly, his eyes glued to the top of a distant line of trees. "Yeah, I'm a farmer. A goddamn cotton farmer, one of those poor sons-o'-bitches in business with God. But we're fully integrated," he continued in a more familiar tone. "We're primarily cotton merchants; we buy from farmers and sell to the mills. Do a lot of exporting—we have offices on each continent. I'm the fourth generation to run it; my father passed away three years ago. Alcoholic," he stated, his eyes suddenly searching Richard's.

Again they fell silent, Warwick's gaze returning to the distant trees. Richard felt an embarrassment, having heard something perhaps he shouldn't have heard. His own father had done just about every kind of honest labor he could find to hold his family together. He farmed their small acreage and performed heavy carpentry all over the county. He even took the night shift at a knitting mill when Richard won the track scholarship to East Tennessee State. He had died of overwork.

"But don't let that worry ya, friend," Warwick yawned. "I get the job done. Our only duty right now is to kill a few innocent, peace-loving birds. Silly thing for Christian folk to do, isn't it?"

Richard began to feel more comfortable with Warwick, enjoying the beauty of the countryside and the chance for introspection. He felt relieved, allowing his mind to wander from the law and the insecurity of his new position—something he wished he could do more often.

The morning eased toward noon, the still air warming and small cumulus clouds clustering in the sky. But nothing moved, nothing broke the heavy quiet. Then suddenly a series of muffled booms wafted from the distance. Warwick stood gracefully and concentrated toward the line of trees. He appeared to Richard like a general sensing the commencement of battle.

"Somebody's got some," he said. "It sounds like it's over by the lake. That ought to send them toward us, since they're facing this way."

Richard stood and picked up his shotgun. He broke a box of shells and stuffed them into his pockets. He then cracked his barrel and peered down it for dust. Hunting for him had always been less pleasure than necessity; at home one was taught to shoot for food.

"Stay right at the edge of the shade," Warwick said,

preparing his own firearm. "And remember, let me shoot first. I know how they fly this field."

Suddenly tiny specks appeared over the trees, then more, swooping down again and darting from side to side. Richard heard Warwick clicking shells into his gun. The first several birds veered away from the tree, but the others continued forward. Richard slowly raised his weapon, the urge to fire, to enter into conflict with nature, rising up in his chest. But Warwick waited, his gun raised halfway to his shoulder. The birds came closer and closer, the whir of their wings becoming clearer and clearer. Yet Warwick remained motionless, his mouth pursed and eyes filled with what seemed hatred.

Then suddenly a tremendous boom shook Richard, and automatically he raised his gun and fired—pointing the gun, instead of aiming, as he had been taught—sending out shock after shock. Four birds simply stopped flying and fell with silly flutters slowly to the earth.

Both men moved their hands smoothly yet quickly from pocket to weapon, risking motion against time to reload. The birds scattered throughout the field, flying this way, then that, confused and further confusing their own kind. The two men again raised their guns, as if in planned unison, again sending out great explosions against the disarray. More birds fell with ridiculous, lazy abruptness toward the ground, the flapping of wings and the clamor of shells against metal growing irregular. Richard had no time to think, his every energy forced toward succeeding in the massacre. He knew it was exciting and elating, but continued to move like a machine: loading, raising, firing in perfect discipline.

And then he heard a whirring toward his left, near, nearer than ever before. He started to turn, just as he heard Warwick yelling. He heard the yelling, but didn't hear the word or words. It was only sound, followed by the loudest sound he had ever heard. And he felt his body twitch violently, his own muscles doing something he knew they knew to do, feeling his whole body trying to fly, to go down, to embrace the earth. And he felt heat and pushing and thousands of tiny feelings. And then nothing.

2

RICHARD SHARED A small frame house in an older section of Memphis with a young mortgage banker named Irwin White. The furniture was sparse, and it was hot during the summer. But the rent was right—two hundred dollars a month—and it had a spacious, tree-filled yard and a wide, covered porch.

As the alarm buzzed at six forty-five the next morning, Richard could barely move. His head pounded from too much whiskey, and his skin felt hot and tender from the many small abrasions inflicted by the gunshot. At first he considered calling in sick, but knew he couldn't live with the lie. So instead he stood shakily and stumbled to turn off the alarm. He paused and then made his way to the bathroom. He turned on the shower and sat down on the toilet. Never had he felt so bad. He held his face in his hands despite the pain.

After the shower, he shaved carefully, grimacing as he scraped the right side of his face. Afterward he stared at himself in the mirror. The little wounds looked like acne—thank God none of the pellets had hit his eyes. He treated the spots with an ointment a doctor at the hunt had given him, then returned to the bedroom to dress. The starch in his shirt rubbed the spots on his neck, so he decided not to tighten his tie until he got to the office. It was then that he remembered Irene, and a wave of energy passed through his body. She was so attractive and had been so kind after the accident. She had leaned against him in her wet bikini to apply medicine, the damp cloth accentuating the warmth of her soft, delicate skin. And he remembered the smooth, regular breath bathing his face as she concentrated on her task. "Damn," he muttered; it had all been worth it.

He left the bedroom and made his way slowly down the stairs. When he reached the kitchen he found Irwin bent over the morning paper, eating a bowl of cereal.

"Morning," Irwin said to the paper. "How was the hunt?"

"Oh, great," Richard replied, opening the refrigerator and pulling out a jar of orange juice. "Except I got shot."

"You what?" Irwin gasped. "What happened?"

Nothing serious," Richard replied, practicing for explanations he knew he would have to make at the office. "But too damned close for comfort."

"How in the hell did it happen?" Irwin asked, staring through his glasses. "Somebody get mad—or get drunk?"

"Oh, no," Richard answered, putting bread in the toaster. "Some birds came in real near and Warwick pulled around too fast. Thank God we weren't that close to each other—or it might have been worse." Richard brought a bowl to the table and sat down. "Finished with the sports?" he asked.

"Yep," Irwin replied rapidly, twisting his small frame in the chair and reaching for a cigarette. "I told you that

14

guy was nuts. He may make a lot of money, but I still say he's nuts. He killed a kid when we were young. It was an accident—but still. Ran over him with a speedboat. Old man Morgan bought his way out."

"Well, it wasn't a big deal," Richard said, pouring the cream. "And it was a great party, really put on right."

"Oh, yeah," Irwin chuckled, returning to the paper. "Morgan sure knows how to put on a party. Was there any puss around?"

"Oh, most of it looked married," Richard mumbled through the cornflakes. "But Warwick sure had a nice date."

"Who was that?" Irwin asked, flicking his cigarette on the ashtray.

"Irene Moody," he answered. "A real looker."

"Oh, hell," Irwin replied, returning to the newspaper. "That's ol' Sammie's sister."

Richard felt a rebuke and let his spoon descend. "Who's Sammie?" he asked.

"Sammie? He's a bookie in town," Irwin answered to the paper. "Not a bad egg. Did some time in the pen, from what I hear. But still an all-right guy. Real intelligent— for that kind of work."

"But, why...what's a *bookie* doing around Warwick?" Richard asked, the very word repulsive to him.

"Hell, War's a big player," Irwin answered, looking up. "He'll bet anything, 'specially sports. But I guess that's his business—wants to win everything. But still, Sammie's an all-right guy."

15

"And where does Irene fit in?" Richard asked, reluctant to hear the answer. "Is she a bookie too?"

"Oh, hell no," Irwin laughed. "She's . . . she's the *bait*, I'd guess you'd call it. She sure ain't no bookie—not enough brains for that."

Richard returned to his cornflakes, his head beginning to throb again and his spirits descending. He ate a couple of mouthfuls, trusting the cereal would be good for him. Finally he knew he had to ask again.

"What do you mean 'bait'?" he asked, as calmly as he could.

"Oh, a little mud for the turtle," Irwin answered. "A little corn for the turkey."

Richard remained still, his spoon poised, pretending to study the sports page. He felt anger rise up inside him, but knew not its source. He looked at Irwin and his hawk's face. Perhaps Irwin was wrong. Perhaps he didn't like Warwick. But how could he not like that girl? With her openness, her softness, her . . . her perfection? It was painful to him. He would think about it later, when he was more himself.

"Whore's the word, I guess," Irwin tossed off, folding the paper. "You've met a million of 'em—part of the family business. But maybe not; maybe she just likes to screw, or likes rich guys. I don't know. Don't argue with the void, just fill it."

"Okay," Richard announced suddenly. "I'll see you after work. Have a good day."

16

Richard worked in a firm of some thirty lawyers with offices downtown atop a tall bank building. His own office was small and plain, but because he worked for the senior partner, it overlooked the awesome Mississippi River.

The ride to work was painful. The Volkswagen had always been too small for him, and the noise and constant shifting in traffic made his headache worse. He finally arrived and parked, the bright sunshine half blinding his eyes. Inside the modern building it was dark and cool. He rode the elevator with his eyes closed. He could feel the looks of the other riders, but didn't care—he just wanted to get behind his own door.

He strode past the receptionist silently, wondering why anyone would chew gum at eight-thirty in the morning. He reached his cubicle without having to speak with anyone, although a couple of lawyers stopped and turned as they saw him pass. Inside he took off his coat and loosened his tie. He didn't want coffee; perhaps tea would taste better. He turned in his chair and focused on the river. Many times he had looked out at the huge, brown mass, wondering at its mystery. The very existence of something so immense and important—not just to commerce but to nature itself—overwhelmed him. He could sit for hours and stare in simple fascination.

This morning he saw details which were new to him. A sparkling clean Coast Guard vessel eased away from the mouth of the old Wolf River harbor. A huge tree bobbed half submerged near the distant Arkansas bank, having

17

traveled perhaps hundreds of miles. A long tow labored around the great bend to the south, laden with materials essential to the workings of the nation. Most Memphians ignored the river. Like alpine farmers, they grew bored with the majesty so near them, forgetting it was there because it had always been there. But Richard vowed he would become more familiar with this mammoth presence. Despite its dangers, the hidden evils that surely must be there, he wanted to know it, embrace it.

The door opened suddenly, giving Richard a start. It was his boss, Arnold Player, a tall, wiry man with salt and pepper hair and dark blue eyes.

"What in the hell happened to you?" Player asked with a note of concern.

"I went to a dove hunt down in Mississippi," Richard replied, struggling to smile. "Got a little too close to a man arguing with a bird."

Arnold touched his glasses as he examined Richard's face intently. "Looks like you did worse than the bird. Didn't hit your eyes, did it?"

"Oh, no," Richard answered, remembering how lucky he was. "Just feel a little stupid."

"Well, I can use some of your *real* talent this afternoon," Arnold said, squaring his shoulders. "A fellow's coming in with an international tax question about one-thirty. I'll fill you in when you come down."

"Great," Richard responded as cheerfully as possible. "I'll be there."

The door closed, and Richard placed his hands to his

head. How in the world was he going to feel well enough to be intelligent in front of a new client? He was hoping he would be able to stay hidden in his room all day. Suddenly the door opened again, and Richard jerked to the alert. There, to his immense relief, stood Martha, his secretary, a small, pert forty-five-year-old, holding a cup of coffee.

"I saw you come in," she said. "And after twelve years at this fancy establishment, I can spot an associate with a hangover four doors away."

"Thank you, Martha," Richard whispered, sitting up. "But please don't go into last night's prayer meeting. I need the olive branch, not the sword—please."

"I spent last night," she began, shutting the door and placing the coffee on Richard's desk, "practicing my yoga. Then Tom and I watched William F. Buckley on the educational station absolutely annihilate some liberal...*professor*...who wanted to give free medical care to everyone, and I mean *everyone*. Then we had some hot chocolate, read awhile, and went to bed."

Richard stared at her for a moment, then folded his arms and asked, "And what then?"

Martha looked blankly at Richard for several seconds, then blushed. "There you go again—that's all your generation can think about. All your brains are...below your belt."

"I don't know why that's such a bad question," Richard said, reaching for the coffee. "A woman of your looks and allure must have some commerce with the topic."

19

"I love you," she whispered with her eyes closed, "even if you are a profligate. I hope you don't mind my prying, but what's wrong with your face?"

"Well, I met a new girl last night, Martha—"

"That's not true," she shouted. "And don't say things like that. It ruins...it ruins your whole...image."

"Look, Martha," Richard said, replacing his hands to his head. "You won't understand this because you've never had a hangover, but I feel like shit. S-h-i-t. So please lay off. I hurt."

"All right," she pouted, "but you can at least tell me you're all right."

"It was a little hunting accident," he murmured before hearing her gasp. "But it's not serious—she just forgot to shave."

Richard watched the door close and chuckled to himself. He wished all women were like Martha—feminine, understanding, amusing. And then he remembered Irene and wondered if she were fun—if she could laugh and tease and create games. And he stretched back in one great body yawn, his whole being tingling and shooting with energy. He surely wanted to find that out. He surely wanted to see her again.

Arnold Player drummed a wooden pencil against a crystal ashtray on his desk. It was a habit Richard had noticed before, while sitting in the big, tastefully appointed office. It was a technique, Richard had decided, designed to signal to all others, whether fellow lawyers or clients, that his superior mind and gift of concentration were being applied totally to the question at hand. And in the silence, the rat-tat-tat became as commanding as the baton of a great conductor.

The pencil finally dropped, and Arnold turned toward Richard and said, "Richard here is our expert on international matters, particularly with taxation. That's why I asked him to join us. What...what are your first impressions, Richard? Are there any opportunities here?"

Richard knew he was on a new footing with Arnold, simply by the fact that he was invited at this initial stage to sit in with an important client and by the deference he was being shown. He felt he had to be correct, had to be completely professional.

"Well," he said, forcing himself to speak clearly, "I think we're faced here with some very basic problems."

"Issues is probably a better word," Arnold said pensively, flashing a steely glance at Richard. "Issues which have a rather wide latitude."

Richard remembered Arnold's admonition to the associates that they must always be very positive in front of clients, that a great part of the role of lawyer was to give them confidence and to encourage them to proceed with their profitable endeavors.

"Yes," Richard stuttered, wishing to God he hadn't stayed out so late. "But Mr. Speakman is proposing to sell the filter casings made in Thailand back to his U.S.

company. And that's going to render the income over there subject to U.S. taxation, regardless of the tax-haven potential in the host country."

"But it seems to me this is done all the time," the elderly, well-dressed client interjected politely. "Why, look at General Motors and the automobile people. They all send their products back here to be sold."

Richard paused, his head pounding. For a flash he felt nauseated. He prayed he could turn such hesitations into advantage as Arnold could. "That's right, Mr. Speakman, but they're not availing themselves of lower tax rates in the host country. The rates in England and Germany are roughly the same as over here, and the manufacturer gets credit for the European taxes against his liability over here. You want to try to keep the profits overseas and pay the reduced tax burden promised by the Thai government."

Richard paused again and noticed Arnold was turned in his chair and staring blankly at his desk. "You see, you're a controlled foreign corporation while doing business in Thailand because the Thai company is wholly owned by the parent. And you're taxed on any of the profits made on goods sent back to this country for sale."

"Let my family own the Thai company, then," Mr. Speakman said, looking from Arnold to Richard and back. "Let the wife and kids own it."

"Uh, no, sir," Richard replied, seeing from the corner of his eye that Arnold continued to stare at the desk. "That won't work either. You'd be a foreign personal holding company, since . . . since it's a closely held company."

"Then use a straw man or resident agent," Speakman argued, crossing his legs.

"That won't hold up in an audit," Richard countered, desperately wishing he could produce a miracle, some small way to be positive with the client.

"Then use a real gimmick—like a Swiss bank account," Speakman said with finality, turning toward Arnold. "I hear everyone and his brother's got one."

"But that would be a *crime*," Richard almost whispered, before watching Mr. Speakman turn toward him with his mouth slightly opened.

"Well!" Arnold interrupted, turning his chair back toward the group. "I don't think the problem is insurmountable. We'll just have to start doing our homework. Bill, I know you're busy, so let's not hold you up any further. We'll go to work on this thing and be back in touch shortly."

Speakman agreed and rose, along with his assistant. Handshakes and pleasantries were exchanged, and they left. Arnold closed the door behind them and returned to his desk. He picked up the wooden pencil and jabbed the rubber end against the desktop.

"Listen, *goddammit!*" he shouted angrily. "Never—and I mean *never*—use the word *crime* around a client of mine!"

"But, Arnold, it would be a crime to open a Swiss front, and he should know—," Richard sputtered.

"He pays us extremely handsome fees to keep him *out* of trouble," Arnold thundered. "And we're not going to insult him by implying his ideas are felonious. Do you get the picture?"

Richard was thoroughly defeated. He didn't have the strength to argue, and doubt overwhelmed him. He let his head drop. He could say no more.

"I want a good result out of this," Arnold said, pounding the pencil again. "Damned good and damned quick."

"I don't think there's one he'll like," Richard answered, pleadingly.

"No, sir," Arnold responded, standing. "I want one that will work, and one he'll goddamn *like!*"

3

RICHARD SPENT THE remainder of the afternoon in his office, absorbing himself in the
everyday work which always seemed to crowd his desk.
There was a contract from opposing counsel which had to
be read carefully, then a tax-appeal brief he had written
which had to be checked for spelling and citations. There
were a number of telephone calls, each tedious to the point
of irritating. The last was from an officer at the bank who
questioned over and over the wording of an insignificant
section of the master contract with the bank's credit card
affiliate. Richard was tempted to tell the fellow the truth—
that the language in the contract had already been
approved by superior officers and that he was an insignificant functionary whose ideas made no difference. But
Richard felt sorry for the man, sensing he was reaching
out for some assurance of the value of his role at the bank.

Finally it was five-thirty, the earliest an associate could
expect to leave the office. Richard stuffed a few papers into
his briefcase, knowing he would never look at them. He
reached the elevator without incident and rode to the
ground floor. The drive home was hectic, and it was a
relief to turn from the busy thoroughfare onto the quiet
street which ran in front of his house.

Wearily he crossed the front porch and opened the

screen door. Inside it was dark and cool. He headed toward the kitchen and a can of beer. He opened it, threw his coat and tie on the tired old sofa in the living room, and returned to the porch. He fell across the padded swing at one end and gave out a long, audible sigh. He closed his eyes and listened to the wind playing through the newly burnished leaves in the trees surrounding the house. It was a sound that reminded him of fall as a boy and conjured up the smell of trailing smoke and dogs barking pleadingly for an afternoon squirrel hunt in the valley near the house. Was it all worth it? All the work and anxiety and sacrifice? He remembered how it was always Harvard or nothing—an almost impossible burden for a country boy from a secondary college—because it was the only law school that offered a scholarship which paid everything. And then there was the struggle to keep good grades, in order to retain the scholarship. All the other students seemed so glib and well prepared, few of them carrying the burden, and humiliation, of poverty. Wouldn't it have been wiser to have stayed at home and worked for TVA or Alcoa? Maybe he wasn't made for a big-city practice. Perhaps privilege only inures to the privileged.

At that moment Irwin appeared at the screen door wearing nothing but a towel around his waist. "You look kinda whipped," he murmured, rubbing his hair. "Bad day?"

"Hell, yes," Richard mumbled. "Had a big row with Arnold Player—you can guess who won."

26

"I don't think that guy gets laid enough," Irwin sighed. "What's his wife like?"

Richard started to defend Arnold's wife, but stopped himself. He knew Irwin was trying to be encouraging. "Yeah, maybe that's it," he answered.

"Well, I'm taking the world's meanest woman out for a couple of drinks and a pizza," Irwin said, snapping his towel at the arm of the swing. "You wanna come with us?"

"I don't think so," Richard answered. "I'm going to hit the hay pretty early."

"Okay," Irwin shouted, letting the screen slam behind him. "We'll be at Gino's if you change your mind."

Richard lay still in the swing, enjoying the warm glow from the sunset. The grass needed cutting, and leaves were gathering on the driveway. That had always been one of his jobs as a youth, to keep the yard well manicured. But he didn't have the energy to work and drifted off into a half sleep. Soon Irwin spun out of the driveway with a toot of his horn, and he was left alone.

He looked at his watch and realized it was after six. Telephone rates were lower now and he needed to call his mother. He pulled himself off the swing and made his way into the living room. They had just installed direct dialing in her county, so he slowly rolled out the numbers.

"Mother?" he asked as cheerfully as he could. "This is Richard. How y'all doin'?"

"Oh, I'm fine," he said after a pause, keeping his voice raised. "Everything's going along just fine."

He was then quiet for a number of minutes, his eyes wandering around the room, the silence broken only by the occasional yes.

"Well, tell her not to worry about it," he finally said firmly. "If she doesn't get the scholarship, I'll make up the slack. By the way, did you get my last check?"

He heard her reply and murmured, "Good."

There was further conversation about the tobacco cutting and the death of a neighbor. And then, since they both agreed the conversation was becoming expensive, they exchanged affections and hung up. He stared at the telephone a few seconds, then returned to the porch. There's still enough daylight to mow the lawn, he told himself. Maybe that'll make me feel better. Or maybe I should go running; I could use a good sweat.

At that moment the telephone rang and he sauntered inside. It was probably some girl calling Irwin, he told himself. He answered with a dull "hello" and was surprised to hear crackling, popping sounds.

"Hello, big fellow," the distant voice shouted. "Whatcha doin'?"

"Oh, not much," Richard replied, surprised at the echo of his own voice. "Who's this?"

"It's Morgan, you asshole," he heard faintly. "I'm calling from the boat."

"What boat?" Richard asked incredulously. "Where are you?"

"We're out on the Mississippi, up around Tiptonville,"

the voice answered, fading in and out. "This is a radio phone."

"Well, what are you doing?" he asked, a grin spreading across his face.

"We're having a good time, meatball, and we want you to come join us," Warwick yelled.

"I can't do that," Richard shouted into the receiver. "I've got a big case to work on at the firm."

"What kind of case?" Warwick yelled.

"Oh, an international law question," Richard answered, suddenly wishing he could go. "It's about taxes and stuff."

"I want to hear about that," Warwick said faintly. "Where can we pick you up?"

"I can't go," Richard shouted. "It's a big client."

"Maybe I'm a big client," Warwick echoed. "I might need some help in that area."

Richard knew Warwick was putting him on, but it was encouraging. He wanted desperately to be out on the river. It would be fun, exciting.

"We'll pull into the Yacht Club down from your office tomorrow about three-thirty or four," Warwick yelled. "We'll have you back by eight the next morning if you want."

"All...all right," Richard answered hesitantly. "But I've got to be back!"

And then he heard Warwick sign off with his radio number. He hung up the telephone and stared into the growing dimness of the room. Perhaps she would be there, and he could get to know her better. He would find some way to leave early. He would do it.

Richard jumped up from the sofa and whistled up the stairs to take a shower. The hot, steamy water seemed to wash away the cares of the day, even the smell of the soap evoking freshness and new life. Drying himself, he felt a touch of hunger and decided to meet Irwin and his girl at the pizza restaurant. While putting on casual clothes, he thought of what the boat trip might be like: the vast surge of the river, new sounds, and exotic sights. And surely she would be there. After all, she was War's girl. And he could talk with her again, get to know her better. A few minutes later, he climbed into the Volks and made his way toward north Memphis.

It was dark inside the restaurant, but Richard was able to sight Irwin and his girl. At the table he introduced her as Constance and told the waitress to bring a pizza along with another round of beer.

"You may wonder why my roommate looks like he has terminal zit," Irwin whispered across the candlelight. "But it's not that; he just got too close to War Morgan's shotgun."

"Oh, my God," she moaned. "I'm surprised he didn't kill you. He's a real crazy."

"It was just an accident," Richard replied, remembering he would be Warwick's guest the next evening. "It could have happened to anyone."

"To hell with that," she said, brushing back her fluffed, sandy hair. "I've seen him do crazier things than that. Why, I remember him throwing butcher knives at Ardis Neild. He thought it was a big *joke* or something, but she told him to go to hell and left the party."

"Well, he may be a kook," Irwin said, reaching for the newly arrived beers, "but a lot of folks think he's a genius."

"Genius, shit," Constance mumbled, so as not to be heard by the waitress. "He's nothing but a spoiled brat."

"Hell, he's made millions," Irwin continued, taking a long sip, "mostly in the futures market. 'Course having a rich daddy pass away didn't hurt. But you can't take it away from him. Land, oil wells—even a Broadway play— the guy's good. He gave me a tip one night that sure paid off."

"What's that?" Richard asked, a little disappointed in Irwin's taste in women.

"Oh, one night a year or so ago over at the Country Club," Irwin began, "a bunch of the 'regulars' were sitting around the men's bar playing gin—you know, a penny a point or something—and in walks War. He's high as a kite—on whiskey, I guess—and wants to get in the game. Only problem was, he wanted to play for a dollar a point. Well, most of us can't exactly play in that league, so he agrees—with me, Clyde, and Jimmy—to play for five cents, and that's way over my head. Well, after a couple of hands, he leans back and orders another drink. Then he looks at us—and you know that look of his—and says, 'You rubes want to make some *real* money?' Well, we all thought he wanted to go back to that dollar a point crap, so none of us says anything—ol' Jimmy just deals the next hand. Then, when his drink arrives, he takes a long gulp and slams the glass on the table and says, 'Sell December cotton.' We all pick up our cards, of course—we knew what he was saying, but none of us wanted to gamble on cotton futures—but he wouldn't let it alone. He starts shouting, right there in the club, 'Sell December cotton, you fuckin' rubes!' Well, ol' Clyde picks up the first card, and none of us says anything, and we play the hand out. I can't remember who won. But after the game, ol' War pulls a hundred dollar bill out of his pocket—shit, nobody had won or lost more than ten bucks—throws it on the table and weaves out of the room. Well, a couple of older members bitched a little about the language he used, but, hell, that didn't bother us."

Irwin paused, no one caring about the steaming pizza the waitress had just delivered. He took another drink of beer and continued. "Well, the next day I'm riding around looking at lousy real estate deals, and I finally pull into a hamburger joint near Bartlett. And I'm sitting there eating this greasy hamburger, and my stomach starts to hurt. And I think to myself, there must be a better life than this. So I start thinking about ol' War and his 'Sell December cotton.' Well, I get in my car and start toward town. And the more I think about it, the more I decide I might throw a little money at the idea. So I call my stockbreaker—you know ol' Allen—and he tells me not to do it. But I told him my mind was made up, and we shorted a couple of contracts. Well, nothing happened for a week or so, and then the goddamn market broke like there was no more need for Kotex, and I made about seventy-five hundred dollars. Just about the easiest money I ever made. And it happened just like that."

"Damn," Richard muttered in the ensuing silence. "That's a lot of money to make over a card game."

"Yeah, but I eventually gave most of it back," Irwin said, diving into the pizza. "I decided I was a big soybean trader, a genius! Lucky I didn't lose more."

The three continued their meal, the girl throwing out small talk about personalities in Memphis—who was seeing whom and where people were traveling. Irwin told a few anecdotes about his week in business—there was big demand for mortgage money at the time. But Richard kept his thoughts to himself. He was staggered that someone could make seventy-five hundred dollars with such little effort. It was more than half of what he was paid annually. It was almost enough to put one of his sisters through college. And it seemed so certain, as if it were ordained.

Fatigue finally won over, and Richard told Irwin and Constance he wanted to head home. Besides, he didn't want to interfere with their evening. He left the restaurant and drove through the dimmed streets. Seventy-five hundred dollars. In two weeks. If he could do that once a year, his money problems would be solved. At the house he undressed quickly and slid into bed. Tomorrow was going to be a big day. He had to work on the Speakman problem, as well as his regular work. And then he had to figure out a way to leave early. He knew he couldn't tell anyone where he was going—Arnold didn't even like the partners to play golf during the week.

Richard turned himself in bed, stretching and feeling relief that the day had ended more pleasantly. Life was indeed looking up. There would be good events along with the bad. And then he wondered what it would be like moving across the mighty brown waters. And what was Morgan really like? What did he want? But his last thoughts were of the girl, with her long auburn hair and silky white skin. He was going to find out about her too. He was going to go on the trip.

4

RICHARD AWOKE FULLY rested the following morning and sang along to the music on the radio as he showered and dressed. Irwin's room was empty, so he assumed Constance had been more than generous the night before. He picked the *Commercial Appeal* out of a bush in front of the porch and read it over his bacon and eggs. He was tying his tie when he remembered he would have to pack some clothes if he were going on the boat with Warwick. And that's when remorse struck him— leaving work early was a real dalliance, an irresponsibility, in truth. He sat on the side of the bed to think it through. He had only been with the firm less than a year. Arnold liked him, perhaps even respected him, but he had just been given his first rebuke. It wasn't a crisis, but perhaps it wasn't the time to act like a playboy. On the other hand, it was the only chance he had to do those things—see the river, get to know Warwick. See her.

Impulsively he stood and grabbed a small bag. I can always change my mind later, he told himself, as he rummaged for underwear and toothbrush and sweater. I've got time during the day, I'll see how I feel around lunchtime. He finished packing, put on his coat, and whistled out the door. He sped the Volkswagen out the driveway and headed toward the traffic. I'll just let things happen, he told himself, steering into the congestion. I'll see how it looks around three.

Once in his office, Richard whipped off his coat and set about to finish routine matters early, so he could research the Speakman problem. But no sooner had he begun to concentrate than Martha stepped through the door.

"I'm glad to see you looking better this morning," she chirped, placing the coffee service on his desk. "I trust you got to bed early."

"Early and alone," he answered, reaching for the coffee. "I'm sure you approve of that."

"Why, I certainly do, Mr. Liberal," she answered, bending over to inspect the wounds on his face. "What are your politics, by the way? You didn't vote for McGovern, did you?"

"Everybody in east Tennessee is Republican, Martha," he answered, flipping through a file to find a memorandum he had written. "From Civil War days."

"Then you voted for Nixon?" she asked cautiously.

"I'm not braggin' about it," he mumbled, becoming annoyed by her intrusion.

"Well, you're not ashamed, I hope?" she asked, straightening a stack of books on his credenza.

"Martha, I don't think you would accept my explanation," he answered with frustration. "So please let me get to work. I've got lots to do."

"Well, don't get your back up," she cooed. "It's...it's

just that you're so...different...from the other associates."

"Different?" he asked quietly. "How 'different'?"

"Oh, more personable, I suppose," she answered, feeling she had gained his attention. "Something a woman would notice."

"Oh, Martha," Richard moaned, waving his hand, his face reddening.

"Just like now," she giggled. "You're embarrassed—I can see it."

"For God's sake, get the hell out," Richard sputtered, suppressing a smile. "Or we'll both get fired."

Martha left, and Richard returned to his work. He dictated the charter to a new corporation, along with its bylaws and organizational minutes. He then answered lengthy correspondence from an out-of-state attorney regarding documents which would be necessary in Tennessee for the merger of his client's corporation with one represented by the firm. After that he composed a contract wherein a client agreed to repurchase stock owned by a former employee. After each assignment, he dutifully filled in the information on his time-and-work sheet. After a while, he stood and walked to the large plate-glass windows. Down below he could see the sparkling river with endless, verdant cotton fields stretching for miles beyond. Did he have the courage to go? He would see after lunch. Perhaps something would come up which would help him decide.

He ate a hamburger at his desk while returning the calls which had come in during the morning. He then checked his papers and calendar to see if there was any work which could not wait until the next morning. At about one-fifteen he gathered his legal pad and pencils and headed down the long hall lined with secretaries' desks toward the library. The library was a large windowless room in the center of the office complex. It was filled with rows of metal stacks containing court reports and legal services. In the center was an open space with several two-man work tables. It was carpeted and quiet. And it was clearly understood that no one but a partner was supposed to carry on conversation.

There was only one other person in the room at the time—another associate—so Richard chose his table and laid down his pad and pencils. He then proceeded to the stacks and began searching through the Commerce Clearing House tax service. He found the volumes he thought might contain the answers he sought and returned to the table. How in hell am I supposed to do the impossible? he asked himself, while turning toward the "less-developed-country" provisions of the Tax Code. Sometimes you have to tell a client it can't be done. Arnold is the real problem; he doesn't know a damned thing about this area of the law. He finally found the appropriate sections and began straining his eyes to read the small print.

"Whatcha working on?" the associate next to him whispered loudly.

"A tax question," Richard answered without looking up.

"Who for?" the fellow asked, letting his book slide to the desk in preparation for a talk.

Richard looked up and recognized the associate. He had been with the firm for a couple of years. He was from a good school and produced careful work, but his whole approach to the law seemed gutless. He never stuck his neck out; he always covered everything he said with cowardly escapes. Richard noticed he was getting heavy from the sedentary occupation and was losing hair above his moist forehead.

"For a client," Richard answered with a straight face.

"Yeah, but which partner?" the associate asked earnestly.

"Why is that important?" Richard asked, anger welling up mysteriously.

"The review's coming next month," he whispered, his eyes checking the rest of the room. "Let's face it—some partners have more influence than others. Who are you doing that for?"

"Oh, shit," Richard gasped, grabbing his head. "I don't give a hoot who it's for. I'm here to do a good job and be paid for it."

"Yeah, but we're all in the same boat," the associate persisted. "If all of us—"

"No, we're not!" Richard answered loudly, turning toward the associate.

The two stared at each other for several seconds before

returning to their reading. Richard was disturbed by the conversation. He was sitting in a sterile, colorless library while his friends were cruising the wondrous Mississippi. He had no one to talk with—perhaps for the rest of his life—except people like the boring, selfish, small-minded bastard next to him. Why had he spent all that energy struggling for advancement if this was where he was headed, surrounded by people asking too little for too much?

He tried to force himself to read the narrow lines on the crisp, flimsy pages. He had to come up with something, an alternative at least, to the client's flawed idea. But he knew those code sections well, and everywhere he turned there were roadblocks. His eyes and fingers darted through the pages like prey seeking refuge. What was he going to do? How could he fight it?

The Yacht Club was difficult to find, there being no sign or clearly defined entrance. A shaky wooden gang-plank led from the nineteenth-century cobblestones on the old embankment to a shabby steel barge bearing a makeshift clubhouse. On either side, connected by plank walkways, were slanting, decaying boathouses, each painted with a different hue of fading pastel. At the far south end, however, under great metal sheds, deflecting view as well as sun, Richard could make out the lines of serene, gleaming yachts, the like of which he had seen only in magazines.

He paused for a moment, taking in the rich, moist

smells of the river. All was quiet, except for the occasional flutter of a bird or the timid play of water against the corroding metal of the barge. He turned toward the clubhouse and opened its squeaky screened door. Inside it was dark and empty, except for a heavy, middle-aged woman standing behind a small snack bar at the end of the room. Cautiously Richard walked toward her, passing a few old couches and a table filled with faded copies of yachting and sailing magazines. He felt intensely that he was out of place, unworthy.

"I'm supposed to meet Warwick Morgan's boat down here," he said with as much aplomb as he could muster. "Have they gotten here yet?"

"That feller's waitin' on ya," the lady answered with a sharp, country accent. "He's got a bunch of groceries too. Down by the pumps—just go on out."

Richard turned where she pointed and saw a line of old gas pumps through the window. He walked out a side door and spotted a man of about fifty seated casually in a long, specially fitted launch. He was dressed in pressed blue pants and a stiff white shirt with epaulets and was reading a newspaper. The man looked up and folded the paper. "You Johnson?" he asked, straightening up.

"Yeah," Richard replied, walking forward.

The man stood and reached for Richard's valise. He then extended his other hand to help him aboard. "Wear this," he said, handing Richard a life vest. "There's not much wind, so we shouldn't get wet."

The man turned and started the powerful engine. He

then walked toward the front to untie the bow. Richard started to ask if he could help, but sensed he shouldn't. Instead he took a seat on a soft, padded bench in the middle. The driver returned to the helm and eased the engine into reverse. The craft slid to the middle of the narrow harbor before the driver shoved the engine into forward. They then glided slowly toward the river, passing the enormous boathouses which grudgingly gave up view of the stately, wondrous yachts inside.

Once at the mouth of the harbor, the driver shouted, "Hold on!" and pressed the throttle forward. The great launch surged toward the west and immediately met the challenge of the mighty current. Richard could feel the force lifting the boat up and pressing it downstream. "They moved the channel over to this bank when they started the new bridge!" the driver shouted over the roar of wind and engine. "You've really got to put the wood to her comin' out! I'm goin' toward the other side where it's a bit slower."

Richard clutched the arm of the bench as the launch bucked against the brown, almost magenta flood. From his seat the distant bank seemed miles away, but the boat sped faster and faster, barely skimming across the swollen waters. There was no other traffic on the river, but Richard could see the occasional bob of a log or the limb of a submerged tree. He knew that contact with one of those could rip the bottom of the craft in an instant. At the very least it could foul the propeller.

But the driver was apparently an old hand at river travel

and safely guided the launch toward the western bank. The ride slowly became smoother, and Richard began to relax. "Want a beer?" the driver yelled. Richard nodded deeply, and he reached into a cooler to produce an imported bottle. Richard took the beer and opened it with his knife. He then balanced himself and took a long, stinging draft. Here he was racing across the giant Mississippi River drinking a beer and feeling the clean, new air of adventure. And all those other jerks were whispering away in their libraries and cubicles, worrying about clients and cases and promotions. To hell with 'em, he told himself, leaning back and shutting his eyes. I've never been able to do this, and I want to do it. I love this feeling, the tingling that comes from danger and speed and elation. This is why I've worked so hard to escape the poverty of my childhood. This is what I've always wanted!

The boat sped past the new bridge, and Richard swiveled around to examine the awesome pylons standing impervious to the power of the river. It filled him with a new sense of the greatness of mankind, its strength and bravery. There is a mastery over nature, he told himself. We are truly what we want to be. There are no real limits, only those that we impose on ourselves.

And then he saw the seemingly limitless levees—huge mounds of earth, ofttimes surfaced with concrete revetment. And he wondered at the time and skill and effort that produced such monuments. About that time, the driver yelled he was moving toward the other side of the channel. A large tow—a boat with a long line of barges in front—was coming downstream, and there would be more room on the other side. "The tow can't stop for several miles," he explained. "It's a little dangerous crossing her bow, but it's still safer on the other side." And he spun the launch toward the east, away from the dazzling sun.

At midstream, Richard looked toward the bow of the tow some two hundred yards away. If the engine failed at this point, they would be caught in the middle of its path. But he felt no fear. If something should happen, he felt he could outswim it, outswim the awful crush of the forward-slanting bow of the lead barge and the powerful suck of the undertow. One needn't worry about the whir of the propellers—he would be drowned by then.

As they reached the other side, Richard stared at the long tow. It was composed of empty gas barges, since they each had a myriad of valves and outlets on top and were riding high in the water. As the boat itself passed, it gave a sharp blast from its horn, and he waved along with the driver. He saw a young man about his own age leaning against the railing of the second deck. How different were their lives; that could be he standing there at the railing, lonely, facing another week of emptiness before reaching New Orleans. But he wasn't going to let that happen. He was going to stay free and determine his own destiny.

As time passed, Richard relaxed and laughed to himself, each bend in the great river bringing forth new sights for feast. The only sounds were of engine and wind, until suddenly the driver shouted, "There she is! There's the *Mary Ann!*" Richard looked up, and anchored behind a sandbar ahead was the largest yacht he had ever seen. It must have been a hundred fifty feet long. It even had a smokestack. "We're about to take her down to the Islands!" the driver shouted. "But Mr. Morgan wanted one more run. She's a beauty, ain't she?"

And Richard's mouth parted. He felt a mixture of anticipation and anxiety, since he couldn't imagine that someone he knew could own such a boat, such a *thing*. His eyes stung, and he had to blink. And the *Mary Ann* let out a long, shrill blast from her mighty horn.

5

IT WAS ABSOLUTELY still at the stern, there being only a tiny rush of current along the water line. Richard leaned back in his cushioned chair and looked toward the west. The sun had taken its leave, but in parting had thrown up garlands of orange and purple and pink against a few puffy bits of cloud. Swallows played and dipped over the water.

"Is it this way every night?" Richard asked quietly, lifting his glass. "I don't think I've ever seen a sunset so beautiful."

"Not every night," Warwick answered absently. "But this is a good way to see it." And then after a pause, "And a good reason to get rich, I suppose."

Richard took a long sip without leaving the dying blaze. Warwick had never referred to his wealth before, and it seemed out of character.

"Tell me about this international law stuff," Warwick asked pleasantly, stretching his long legs in front of him. "I'm interested in that."

"Most of it involves taxes," Richard answered, remembering with discomfort that he hadn't found an answer to the Speakman case. "There are a lot of benefits to doing business overseas, but it's very complicated to do it within the law."

"How do I get a bunch of money out of the country?" Warwick asked.

"For what purpose?" Richard asked.

"For any purpose," Warwick answered. "It's *my* money."

"Just tell your bank to open an account in, say, Switzerland and transfer the money," Richard said. "As long as you leave it in dollars, there's no difficulty."

"Why dollars?" Warwick asked, squinting at his foot with one eye. "Why not francs?"

"I don't think Swiss banks are allowed to pay interest on foreign-held franc accounts," Richard answered. "But I'd have to look that up."

The two fell silent for a few moments, Richard wondering whether Irene was on board. He kept peering through the huge sliding glass doors for signs of life, but saw none. He wondered whether she and Warwick were lovers, whether he would see her again and talk with her privately.

"Now, suppose," Warwick started slowly, "I don't want anybody to know it's there. Suppose I want it there for *emergencies?*"

"That would be impossible," Richard answered nervously, remembering Arnold's rule. "The transfer of any large amount of money out of the country has to be reported to the government. Furthermore, a taxpayer has to report all foreign bank accounts in his tax return each year."

"Yeah, but if it were already *out,*" Warwick said, sitting

up quickly, "there's no way for the bastards to know, is there?"

"Well, the Swiss certainly wouldn't tell them," Richard answered cautiously. "The secrecy laws are pretty tough."

"That's what I heard," Warwick said, crushing his beer can and tossing it over the side.

The two again fell silent, but Richard was concerned with what Warwick was contemplating. He felt compelled to warn his friend of the consequences.

"I...I don't want to mislead you," Richard stammered. "But it's...it's strictly...illegal to transfer the money out or to keep a Swiss account without reporting it."

"Illegal?" Warwick asked quietly, his face betraying emotion. "What the shit's illegal? Goddamn Vietnam was illegal. Betting on football games is *illegal*. Writing off this fucking boat is *illegal*. Our whole goddamn government is *illegal!* I'm just worried about getting caught! You know how much I'm supposed to pay those socialist assholes every year?" he shouted, leaning over. "Almost seventy-five percent of everything I make. And you call that *legal?* I risk my capital, use my God-given talents and hard work, and some nobody jerk in Washington—who doesn't know his ass from a hole in the ground—wants to take seventy-five percent? *Never,*" he hissed.

Warwick paused, and Richard felt embarrassed by the sudden outburst. But oddly he felt flattered Warwick would open up and reveal his emotions. He felt compelled to respond.

"I'll agree it's probably not totally fair—," Richard started.

"*Fair?*" Warwick shouted, standing. "*Fuck fair!* I'm going to tell you how fair those bastards are—they plan to take it all. They're going to turn this country into another England. And when they do that, it's all over. There'll be nobody left to do the work. Nobody left to do the fightin'. It'll be all over. It's then a question of time—months or weeks—before we simply negotiate. Negotiate the surrender, with a gun to our heads. That's why I want some money out. It'll at least give me a little time—a place to go, maybe. And . . . and I'm going to do it."

Warwick stepped to the doors and slid one open. "I'm going to wake up Sammie and play some gin," he said, his voice returned to normal. "Why don't you go talk to Irene in the galley?"

"Fine," Richard answered, trying to conceal his elation. "I'll be there in a minute."

Warwick closed the door behind him, and Richard stared at the flawless teak deck. He would find out Irene's relationship with Warwick before he tried to get any friendlier with her. Besides, there was what Irwin had said about her and her brother. He stood and walked to the doors. He slid one open and walked inside.

A wave of cold air engulfed him, as he closed the door behind him. It was dark inside, but he could make out the features of the main saloon. The floors were inlaid oak, covered with a rich Oriental carpet. A lacquered card table with four chairs was placed near the doors. At the other end of the room was a carved, wooden fireplace with chintz-covered couches on either side. Expensive paintings adorned the walnut-paneled walls.

He walked carefully toward a door to one side of the fireplace. He opened it and entered the dining room. An eighteenth-century English table with six chairs filled the center of the room. There were more beautiful paintings on the walls and glistening silver on side tables. He walked around the table and pushed a door in the corner. It was bright inside the modern galley. Irene was standing at a counter, her face turned away. She was wearing gray silk slacks with a rust-colored sleeveless blouse. She was standing barefooted, one foot tucked pointed behind the other.

"Oh!" she gasped playfully when she saw him. "You scared me."

"I'm sorry," Richard replied, not knowing what to do with his hands. "I should have knocked."

"Dinner'll be ready in a minute," she said, her smile bursting forth. "I hope you like roast beef and baked potato."

"Sure do," Richard replied, once again intoxicated by the smile and the eyes. "Need some help?"

"One of the crew's supposed to set the table," she answered, turning. "Why not fix a drink and just sit on that stool."

As she turned Richard noticed that the silk pants mirrored even the faintest movements of her skin beneath. He realized he was staring and turned to the bar.

"You want something?" he asked, putting ice in a glass.

"I've got a glass of wine somewhere," she answered, looking around.

"I see it," Richard said, grabbing a wine glass from the counter. "Red or white?"

"White," she answered absently, returning to her salad dressing.

Richard poured the drinks and moved to the stool. Once again he became enslaved by the silk and the lustrous hair. He reminded himself of what he had decided on deck and took a long drink from his bourbon.

"How long have you been out?" he asked. "And where have you been?"

"We've been out ever since the hunt," she answered, pouring the dressing on the salad. "We've been up as far as Cairo. We're going to take you back to Memphis tomorrow—unless you want to stay longer."

I wish I could stay forever, Richard said to himself. But he knew there would be even more trouble if he weren't back early. "I don't think I can," he answered, shaking his head.

"I was hoping to hear from you," she said, carefully removing the roast from the oven. "I was afraid you didn't have a very good time on the hunt."

"Oh, no!" Richard sputtered. "I had a great time. But...but I didn't know whether to call or not."

"Why not?" she asked, turning toward him.

"Well I didn't know whether you were War's girl or what," he answered, his mouth trying to form a smile.

"Oh, that's silly," she said, returning to the roast. "It's just like one big family around here."

Confused, yet encouraged by the answer, Richard stood and poured another drink. He returned to the stool and stirred the drink with his finger. He felt on firmer ground, but one could never tell. He was wondering what to say next, when the dining room door opened and a small, white-coated Oriental announced, "The table is ready, Missy."

"Okay, Chop," she replied. "Ring the dinner bell. We'll serve as soon as everyone's seated."

"Where, uh, where can I reach you?" Richard asked, once the servant had left.

"Over at War's house in Memphis," she answered, picking the potatoes out of the oven with a long fork.

Richard noticed that as Irene moved, her hair swung pendulously. Everything about her seemed serene and refined. Irwin must have been wrong—people oftentimes jump to false conclusions.

"Mind picking up that roast?" she asked, herself carrying the salad and potatoes. "There's no sense waiting on Chop."

They proceeded to the dining room where Warwick and Irene's brother were already seated. The two were finishing their gin game, while Chop was pouring wine.

"Have you met my brother Sammie?" Irene asked Richard, while placing her dishes on the table.

"No, I haven't," Richard replied, setting the roast on the table and extending his hand. "Nice to meet you."

"Hi'ya doin'?" Sammie replied gruffly, with a rough smile.

Sammie was a thickly built man of medium height. He had reddish blond hair cut short over a square face. Tender blue eyes stood out in sharp contrast to severely pocked skin. He was perhaps thirty years old and had the presence of a powerful animal which had been at some time mistreated.

Warwick and Sammie continued to play cards during dinner, while Richard and Irene were left to themselves to converse. Finally, over souffle, Richard found a way to include Sammie in the conversation.

"Where are you and Sammie from?" he asked, looking briefly toward the end of the table.

Irene looked up to see if Sammie wanted to answer and then replied, "A little town in Alabama—Troy. Ever hear of it?"

"Sure," Richard replied, not sure whether he had or not, but glad she was from a small community like himself.

"It's where Troy State is," she continued. "That's where Sammie and I went to college."

"Really?" Richard answered, feeling more certain Irwin was wrong. "What did you study?"

"Sammie studied music," she replied. "I only went for two years. I took a bunch of practical courses—you know, home economics, secretarial sciences, that sort of thing."

"All right!" Warwick shouted suddenly, placing both hands on the table. "We're going back to finish off this match. Sammie's got six thousand dollars of mine, but he knows in his heart of hearts he's a loser. Right, Sammie? It shouldn't take me longer than all night to get my money back!"

Everyone chuckled, and the two cardplayers stood and left the room. Richard glanced at Irene as she instructed Chop to clear the table. She then stood and carefully blew out the candles.

"Need any help with the dishes?" he asked, noticing the silk pants anew.

"Chop can do that," she replied, reaching to pick up an ashtray.

Richard stood and walked over to inspect one of the paintings on the wall.

"Want to sit out on the stern?" he asked, leaning over to inspect the tiny brushmarks.

"The entire mosquito kingdom is out there waiting for us," she answered, suddenly bursting into laughter. "But we can watch television or play some music."

"Either sounds fine to me," Richard said, following her into the galley.

Irene busied herself momentarily helping Chop organize the dishes. Richard spied a bottle of wine and found two clean glasses. She then wiped her hands and turned toward him. "Oh, fine," she said, taking the glasses and pushing against another door. Halfway through she stopped and grabbed his hand with hers. Richard was surprised, until she said, "The switch is burned out in the hall, so watch your step."

The two groped down the blackened hallway, Richard clutching Irene's velvet hand. "Now here are some steps," she whispered before descending. Richard followed, almost losing his balance in the darkness. Suddenly she opened a door and light flooded forth. They emerged into a large, comfortably appointed room with a king-sized bed against one wall and a couch with chairs at the other.

"Gee, this is cozy," Richard said, looking around.

"This is my favorite room on the boat," Irene answered. "I feel like I'm hidden away from everything in the world."

Richard put the wine bottle on the coffee table and sat down on the couch, while Irene turned on the television. She twisted the dial several times, finding only two clear channels.

"Well, it looks like a situation comedy and a National Geographic special on ants," she said laconically.

"I'll go for the ants," Richard replied, slipping off his deck shoes.

"It beats mosquitoes," she said, again with a burst of laughter.

She sat down beside Richard on the couch and reached for a cigarette on the coffee table.

"I didn't know you smoked," Richard said with a slight frown.

"Oh, I don't really," she replied, igniting the lighter. "Just after dinner or with something to drink."

"Where do you work?" Richard asked, leaning back in the corner of the couch and placing his hands behind his neck.

"I was a stewardess for Delta for a while," she answered, pouring the wine. "Then I came up here to live with Sammie after my mother died. I had a couple of jobs, but nothing I really liked. I went back to school for a while at Memphis State. I'm really not doing anything now."

Richard watched her eyes as she spoke. They would move slowly from object to object, only occasionally truly focusing. When she stopped speaking, she carefully brushed her hair back with one hand, her eyes looking out into nothing. Richard stood without speaking and walked to the television. He turned it off and slid a tape cartridge into its receiver. A quiet bossa nova filled the room. He returned to the couch and bent over her. She continued to stare into space as he brushed her lips with his. She then came alive as he slid next to her, putting her arms around his back. Her embrace was much stronger than he had expected, her slender body pressing with fervor and her lips searching his face.

Richard stood and lifted her gently. He turned off the lights on either side of the couch and led her toward the bed. As he reached for the buttons of her blouse, his hands met hers. She glanced at him a moment and then began unbuttoning them herself. Richard took off his own shirt and pants and turned to open the bed covers. As he turned around, she pressed against him naked, her arms covering her breasts. He turned off the bed lamp and felt her still pressing as they knelt together into the bed. As he pulled up the covers, he felt the whole length of her softness melt against his body. He found her face in the darkness and then ran his hand along her back and then her buttocks and legs. He felt himself against her stomach as they kissed and explored. With his hand he found her source and felt her legs part. And with her help, he entered, trembling.

6

RICHARD SAT AT the edge of the tattered sofa tying the laces of his running shoes. He had a date with Irene at seven and wanted to run before meeting her. He felt the need to purge himself of the tension and bitterness he had accumulated during the day.

"What did you tell him?" Irwin asked, popping a beer can.

"I told him we were out fishing and lost our engines," Richard answered, his head pounding. "He then started screaming about not calling in. Damn, I thought he was going to fire me right there."

"You should have told him you were sick," Irwin said, leaning against the door jam. "There's nothing wrong with lying to a jerk like that."

"Well, I told him I was out there trying to line up some business," Richard replied, standing. "That calmed him down—he's always preaching about bringing in clients. Still, it makes you feel pretty small. What the hell's wrong with taking a day off?"

"Just lie to 'em," Irwin said, turning toward the kitchen. "Just lie to the bastards."

Richard pulled a jersey over his head and walked out into the fall air. The days were getting shorter, but it was still warm enough to run in shorts. He trotted down the driveway, establishing a gait. He wasn't going to push it, just loosen up and give his body a chance to move and sweat. He reached the sidewalk and decided to run through Overton Park a couple of blocks away. He crossed Poplar Avenue, dodging the traffic, and began running down the center of the golf course. Slowly the roar of the traffic and the city receded, the giant oak and hickory and walnut, resplendent in their autumn foliage, serving as a towering and friendly audience to his efforts. He then began to relax, allowing his arms to move freely and effortlessly. His legs felt firm and graceful, their summer tan not having fully faded. He began to feel himself again, as if he were an old friend, trustworthy and good.

He was also running for her. She had obviously liked his body, shyly touching and feeling it all over, as if it were something new and wonderful and mysterious. He wanted his body to be perfect, in order to please her and to nourish her childlike curiosity. Irwin had to be wrong—surely she had never touched a man's body before.

His thoughts then turned to Arnold and the events of that morning. A sense of guilt overwhelmed him, but that quickly turned to anger. He had been treated like a child and had been humiliated. It wasn't the circumstance of law practice he had always envisioned at Harvard. It was so restrictive, so emasculating. But that would certainly improve; in time Arnold would give him more latitude. He would be accepted.

It was growing dark, but he knew he could make his

way along the soft grass of the fairways without tripping. He ran for several more minutes, then turned and headed toward home, feeling the perspiration on his forehead evaporate in the heavy air. The exercise was doing its magic; his spirits were lifting and the cares of the day leaving. And he was going to see her.

Warwick's home was located in a community several miles east of the limits of the city. To the stranger it would seem just another sleepy west Tennessee village. But most of the area was comprised of magnificent estates hidden behind the simplicity of lacy woods and tranquil, white-fenced pastures.

Richard proceeded slowly down the winding asphalt roadway, his lights turned high. Then on the left he saw the simple split-rail entrance with the diamond-shaped red reflector which had been described to him. He turned into the driveway and felt his wheels cross a cattle guard. He then passed over a thin rubber line, which must have been a security device. He proceeded through a dense forest for perhaps a half mile before he saw lights in the distance. He heard the barking of dogs.

As he came closer he could make out a stately two-storied New Orleans-style home with a circular drive in front. Two large gray German shepherds paced nervously near the front door. He rounded the drive and came to park facing the entrance. He turned off his lights and waited; he wasn't going to leave the car with the dogs so near.

Shortly he saw an elderly black man in a white serving jacket appear at a sidelight. He vanished quickly and then opened the massive door. The dogs turned toward him as he yelled an order. They then wheeled and trotted off into the darkness.

Richard stepped cautiously from the car, feeling for the first time a drop of rain. He walked up the brick steps and said, "I'm Richard Johnson—good evening."

"Please come in, Mr. Johnson," the old man answered softly, stepping back and extending the door. "They're all in the back watching television."

Richard followed down a long, high-ceilinged hallway toward a set of tall, paneled doors. The black man opened them quietly and nodded him inside. Richard stepped through the doors and quickly smelled the aroma of an open fire. He looked up toward the vaulted ceiling, marked with archaic silent fans, and then scanned the spacious, casual room. It was filled with colorful wicker furniture set on top of hand-molded, terra cotta tiles. It was a comfortable room, during any season; sparse, yet inviting.

At first Richard saw no one—a color television was playing noisily in front of one of the many glazed French doorways leading outside. Characters in a situation comedy spoke inanely between bursts of seemingly hysterical laughter. He walked across the room and switched it off.

As soon as the noise evaporated, a voice spoke from behind a great wicker chair at the far end of the room. "Thank God somebody stopped that shit," Warwick's

61

voice boomed. "I had forgotten where it was coming from." Warwick then appeared and walked across the room with his book. "You should have stayed the rest of the day," he said, extending his hand. "We killed a bunch of fish after we let you off."

"I wish I could have," Richard replied with a smile. "But I really caught some grief when I got to work."

"I don't know why you put up with that crap," Warwick growled, placing ice into two glasses. "Tell 'em to kiss your ass."

"Easier said than done," Richard answered, with a tinge of shame. "It's the only job I've got."

"We can always take care of that," Warwick said, looking him in the eye. "Is Scotch all right?"

"Sure," Richard answered, accepting the drink and wondering what the comment meant. Richard also wondered whether Warwick knew he had slept with Irene. He didn't mind competing for a girl, but not with someone who was becoming his friend.

"Whatcha doing tonight?" Warwick asked, walking toward the couch in front of the fireplace.

"Oh, I thought I'd see if Irene wants to take in a movie," Richard answered, sitting in a chair.

"Whatcha going to see?" Warwick asked quietly, his eyes turning toward the fire.

"*A Touch of Class* is supposed to be pretty good," Richard replied, sensing Warwick was really looking at him instead of the fire.

"I'm reading an awfully good book," Warwick mumble softly.

Richard paused and then asked, "Really? What's that?"

Warwick froze, his eyes now looking through the fire. For a moment Richard thought something must be wrong. Finally Warwick turned and stared, "It's a history of weather patterns since the Middle Ages," he replied.

Richard started to laugh, but didn't. There was something earnest in Warwick's voice. For a moment Richard thought he might be drunk.

But suddenly Warwick came to life and began grinning. "It's really fantastic," he said standing and walking to pick the book off the bar. "I've been creating a comparison of the patterns in the United States over the past hundred years with what they guess the weather was over the previous several centuries. The sources are sparse, of course, but it all adds up to some very interesting thoughts. The weather was certainly different from today. Growth rings in trees, old Indian lore—all sorts of things—suggest there've been changes."

But then again he fell silent, his eyes riveted to the book. He remained like that for several seconds, until at last he looked up and said, "Irene won't be ready for thirty minutes. Let's run a little errand."

Richard began to protest as politely as he could. He was becoming quite taken with the girl and had many things he wanted to talk about. But Warwick simply waved his long arm and headed toward a door at the end of the room.

"Oh, well," Richard sighed, "the errand shouldn't take long." They walked through an elegant dining room and through a swinging door into the kitchen.

"Jason!" Warwick shouted. "Where the hell are you?"

The servant appeared, wiping his mouth with a napkin. "Tell Miss Irene we're running an errand and'll be back in a few minutes."

"Yassuh, Mr. Warwick," Jason responded, bowing slightly.

Warwick opened a door and descended several steps into a five-car garage. Richard could hear rain pounding against the roof. Warwick opened the door to a large Landrover and climbed inside. Richard followed suit, hearing the garage open automatically. Warwick roared the vehicle backward, the rain pounding against metal. He sped down the winding driveway, adjusting the wipers. He reached the road, sliding as he made the turn. He then startled Richard with a question.

"Would you do some legal work for me?" he asked.

"Why . . . why, sure," Richard answered, holding on to the dashboard. "What kind?"

"I've bought some apartment buildings," Warwick answered, concentrating on the road ahead. "You know, the write-off kind. I need someone to close the deals."

"Sounds fine to me," Richard replied, relieved it had nothing to do with transferring funds overseas. "Where are they?"

"Out in the burbs," he answered, again adjusting the

speed of the windshield wipers. "I'll get you the stuff tomorrow."

"That's fine," Richard said. "But I can send a messenger over."

"No," he answered. "And I'll send a check for the retainer along with it."

Richard was stunned. He was finally a real lawyer. An intelligent and important businessman was coming to him for advice and work. His chest felt good.

Warwick continued to drive very fast, reaching the expressway and heading toward the west. At the airport exit he turned off. But instead of turning toward the modern terminal, he took the opposite ramp. After about a hundred yards he pulled up in front of an older, gray concrete building with an entrance marked United States Weather Service. He opened his door and dashed toward the canopy. Richard remembered he had no raincoat, but simply mumbled and followed suit.

Inside there was a large two-storied room with curved staircases leading up each side. Warwick took the one to the left two steps at a time. At the top was a sign with an arrow which said Weather Room. Richard followed Warwick's long stride down the hallway and through a door into a brightly lighted room painted a uniform color of light green.

"Hi'ya' doin', goodlookin'?" he shouted to a heavy middle-aged woman sitting at the reception desk. She looked up from her newspaper without a reply. Warwick proceeded straight toward a large table holding huge volumes of computer material. He grabbed one of the heavy tomes and flipped its pages toward the back. He reached the section he wanted and began reading it intensely. After a few moments, he looked toward a group of men sitting together at the other end of the room and asked loudly, "How old is this Texas stuff?"

"Oh, it came in a couple of hours ago," a younger, heavy-set fellow answered softly. "Look up at the top right of the page."

Warwick studied the material for several more seconds, while Richard looked around the sterile, noisy space. He felt he was in a newsroom or a hospital operating room. Finally Warwick let the volume fall with a sound and proceeded toward a wallboard filled with numerous meteorological maps. He studied the maps with his hands on his hips, his teeth biting his lower lip.

"Looks like it's headed toward Louisiana, doesn't it?" Warwick asked without turning around.

No one replied, so Warwick meandered across the room, looking and fingering objects along the way. Richard noticed his patterned, cashmere jacket was virtually soaked. He approached a man sitting before a teletype machine and leaned over to see what he was writing. He then turned his face and looked very closely at the man's eyes and nose and mouth. "That shit's headed east, isn't it?" he whispered.

"Well, Central doesn't think so," the man answered, concentrating on his fingers, "but it sure looks like it to me. Everything looks like it's coming this way, but it's moving too fast to say."

"When do you think it'll get here," Warwick whispered again.

"Hard to say," the man answered, looking away to find a cigarette. "Should be Saturday or Sunday."

"Lotta moisture?" Warwick asked softly, straightening up.

"If it keeps moving this fast, it ought to be a ballbuster," the man replied, lighting the cigarette.

Warwick then turned and waved Richard toward the door. On the way out he leaned over the receptionist's desk and said, "In your next life, you're going to be a beautiful young Indian princess." The woman stared at him without expression and returned to her newspaper.

The two trotted down the hall and then down the stairway. They paused a moment at the entrance and then raced toward the Landrover. Warwick started the machine and raced it toward the expressway. The rain was coming harder than ever.

"What's all that about?" Richard asked, gripping the dashboard again.

"That, friend, is what I do for a living," Warwick answered, adjusting his rearview mirror. "You see, most of the cotton hasn't been picked; it's still sittin' out there in the fields. Now, if we keep gettin' rain like tonight—and even more coming up from Texas—they'll never get the stuff out. The whole crop might be damaged."

"Well, what can you do about it?" Richard asked with concern. "How are you going to get it out?"

"That's not the question," Warwick answered with a sigh. "We started pickin' two weeks early—they thought I was nuts. It's the other assholes who are in trouble."

"Then what's the big worry?" Richard asked.

"To fleece the bastards!" Warwick shouted with a burst of laughter. "It's not a problem. It's an opportunity! Sure, I might lose part of my crop, but that's peanuts compared to what we can make on the entire crop."

"How's that?" Richard asked, watching the slick highway speed past.

"You buy the futures in New York," Warwick answered quietly. "They think this is a bumper year. But if you can't get it out of the fields, it ain't worth a dime. Prices this winter'll go sky-high—that's my bet."

"But if you're right, who'll sell it to you?" Richard asked.

"The idiots who don't know it's raining!" Warwick answered, again bursting into laughter. "No, really, from the people who can't see the changes in the weather. There's something strange going on, particularly this year. It seems the basic airflow is moving. If it's really happening, it'll cause havoc with farming."

The two rode in silence, each watching the rain race across the headlights. It all sounded rather grandiose, but he remembered Irwin's story of the seventy-five hundred dollars. Besides, it was exciting to be around someone who thought in such big terms. It was certainly different from

68

the conversations heard in his firm's library. It was innervating fun.

The garage door opened automatically as Warwick wheeled the Landrover around the circle. As they pulled inside, the assault of the rain ceased, as if magically. The two left the vehicle and walked inside.

"Where's Irene?" Warwick asked the servant, sitting at a counter.

"She gone," the old man replied laconically.

"She's *what?*" Richard asked, stunned and outraged.

"Yassuh," the man replied, slowly bending off the stool. "She left a little while ago. Didn't say a word where she was headed. She took the Buick."

7

"TWO THOUSAND DOLLARS?" Arnold asked for the second time. "What the hell does he want you to do?"

"He wants me to close the deal on two or three apartment complexes he's bought," Richard answered. "And I think there might be some more business behind that."

"Well, let me tell you something about those Morgans," Arnold said, chewing on a pipe. "They didn't make all that money by being the biggest saints on earth, I guarantee you. So watch your step. I don't want the firm getting involved in any funny business. And I sure don't want a big uncollectible."

"I don't think we need to worry about collecting," Richard answered with a grunt.

"Listen, son," Arnold said warmly. "All those big cotton merchants are the same; they all sooner or later get into trouble. It's kind of a death wish. They can't help it. Now, the Morgans are damned shrewd people—don't get me wrong—especially the grandfather. But the father drank himself to death, and this young one—he couldn't be any older than you—hasn't really proved anything yet. And I've seen it happen to the best of 'em, so be careful."

"I will," Richard answered wearily. "I need to get back to work."

Arnold raised his hand and said, "I'm still not happy with the Speakman matter. "Your solution wasn't what they wanted, so I changed it."

"How did you change it?" Richard asked anxiously.

"They're going to sell the goods in this country through an agency in Switzerland," he answered, thumping his pipe against an ashtray.

"But then they lose the tax advantage," Richard argued. "The profits will be taxed in this country."

"Well, we're going to have the kids own the agency," Arnold continued, "to make sure most of the profits stay overseas."

"But, Arnold, the IRS can see right through—," Richard began to argue.

"What they don't know won't hurt them," Arnold answered.

"Yes, but *we* know," Richard said, his voice quivering.

"Look, son," Arnold said, dropping the pipe in the ashtray. "I've been at this game a lot longer than you have and know a hell of a lot more about the Revenue Service than just about any other lawyer in town. The job is to take care of the client's needs, and that's what I expect from you next time."

Richard forced himself to remain silent, even though anger was surging up inside him. He rose and nodded toward Arnold, then left the room. He walked hurriedly down the hallway, his face in a scowl. He walked into his office and slammed the door. He then sat down, took a deep breath and shouted, "Shit!"

At that moment, Martha opened the door carrying a handful of correspondence. "Did someone call?" she asked with a lilt.

"It's going to get worse than that," Richard fumed. "You may not want to hang around."

"Don't get so upset," Martha cooed. "Mr. Player gets on everyone's case from time to time. I think it's part of his theory of management."

"I don't give a damn," Richard sputtered. "He's an *asshole*."

"Hup! Not *that* one, please," she replied in a higher pitch. "I can take the first one, but not the last one."

"Hell, Martha, it's not right to let a client do things which you know aren't within the letter of the law," Richard argued. "And if you apologize for it, you're part of the same system."

"I was just trying to be nice," Martha murmured while turning toward the door.

"Well, don't go away mad," Richard said softly.

"Well, I am mad," she answered, her voice trembling. "I have one daughter in college and another starting next year. I *have* to work if they're going to get to do all the nice things—nice clothes and trips."

"I'm sorry, Martha," Richard whispered.

"Well, you ought to be," she replied, a tear running down her cheek. "You're young, good-looking, and

72

single. You can do whatever you want. You don't know what it's like to have responsibility."

"Martha, I'm sorry," Richard repeated quietly.

"No, you're not," she replied opening the door a crack. "You may be well mannered and attractive, but I think you're selfish."

They both waited in silence while Martha dried her eyes. She then remembered the papers in her hand and placed them on his desk. She gave him a glance and left the room.

Richard leaned back in his chair and exhaled. First the girl, then the boss, and now the secretary. "What is this shit?" he moaned.

Richard stood in the kitchen holding the telephone with his shoulder while trying to open a beer can. He had tried calling Irene over the weekend and from the office, but each time Jason had said she was out. He had decided against calling again, for he felt perhaps she was avoiding him. But once he got home to the empty house, he changed his mind. She couldn't have changed her affections so quickly, he reasoned.

"Hello," he said suddenly, almost losing the telephone. "May I speak with Irene?"

"She still not home," Jason replied. "She s'pose to be back anytime, though."

"Is...is Warwick there?" Richard asked hesitantly.

"One moment, suh," Jason answered.

Richard took a long sip of beer while he waited.

Suddenly Warwick came on the line with a brisk, "Hello, Rich."

"War? How you been?" Richard asked, glad to hear he was in a cheerful mood.

"Couldn't be better," Warwick answered quickly. "Looking for Irene?"

"Yeah," Richard replied. "I haven't talked with her since Friday night."

"She went to a hunt in Arkansas with Sammie," Warwick replied. "I don't know where she is now, but she's supposed to be back."

"Well, have her call me," Richard said, deciding he was beginning to look a little foolish.

"Sure will," Warwick answered, "Whatcha doing now?"

"Getting over another crappy day," he replied, his spirits sinking further. "Arnold won't get off my case."

"What you need is another little trip," Warwick said. "What do you think?"

"Fishing's out of the question," Richard replied. "Hell, I almost got fired the last time."

"No, this'll be different," Warwick said. "I've got to go to New York tomorrow to the Cotton Exchange. Why don't you come with me—as my attorney?"

"Why...do you really need an attorney?" Richard asked.

"You never know," Warwick answered with a chuckle. "New York's a dangerous place."

"The, uh, per diem is kinda high," Richard said.

"Just send the bill, ol' buddy," Warwick interrupted. "Be out at the private air terminal around six in the morning. And, oh, pack a few things. We might have to stay over."

"Sure, sure," Richard replied, still a bit amazed. "I'll be there."

"I'll have Irene call you," Warwick said dryly and then hung up.

Richard replaced the receiver and stared at the beer can. Hell, business is business, he thought to himself. Arnold can't get mad about that. He then walked into the living room and fell onto the couch. The light drizzle outside had made the house dark, so he turned on a lamp. As soon as he turned the switch, the bulb popped and went black. So he pulled himself up wearily and turned on another one. At that moment the telephone rang. He hurried into the kitchen and picked it up. He tried to make his "hello" sound as casual as possible.

"Richard?" the voice said. "It's Irene."

"Why, hello!" he said. "Where have you been?"

"I've been at the doctor's all day," she answered. "Very exciting."

"I've called you several times," Richard said, fairly sure she wasn't mad at him.

"Yes, I know," she replied. "But I didn't want to bother you at the office."

They both paused until Richard said, "I hope you're not sick."

"Oh, no," she said cheerfully. "Just a checkup. How have you been?"

"Great," Richard said, grinning. "Say, why don't we get something to eat? You hungry?"

"Actually, I think I could eat a horse!" she replied. "I haven't had a thing all day."

"Great. I'll be right out to pick you up," he said.

"That's too far," she replied. "You've got to get up early for work. Where'll we meet?"

"Bill and Jim's okay?" he offered.

"See you there in about an hour," she said cheerfully.

Faint ribbons of light from the street lamp outside crept through cracks in the Venetian blinds into the bedroom. Strands of smoke from Irene's cigarette swam through them slowly like seaweed at great ocean depths. The sound of the rain had diminished to careless drippings and pingings.

Richard lay naked in the bed. He felt no compunction to speak or cover himself. He knew Irene now, not every detail, but certainly to the depths that lovers must. He rolled over on his elbow and slid his hand under the sheets to find her stomach.

"I like you," he whispered slowly, still fearful of using "love."

"Hmmm," she cooed, placing her cigarette in the ashtray and sliding down to meet his face. They kissed tenderly, barely touching.

"Why?" she whispered playfully.

"Your hair," he answered hoarsely, burying his face in its silky lengths.

"What else?" she asked with a giggle.

"Your eyes," he answered with disinterest, moving to kiss one of them.

"Is that all?" she asked, moving her head.

"Oh, no," he answered slowly, his hand gliding through the sheets.

The two embraced and lay together without motion, each perfectly content. Finally he returned to his elbow and spoke.

"Have a nice weekend?" he whispered.

"Oh, it was kind of boring," she answered, shifting.

"Well, why did you go?" he asked.

"Oh, to be with Sammie," she whispered with a yawn.

"But you're with him all the time," he probed.

"Yes, but he was over there to play a big game," she answered. "And that gets pretty lonely."

"Can I ask you a question?" he asked.

"Sure," she answered, her head moving.

"Do you and Warwick have a..a *thing?*" he asked uncertainly.

There was a long pause until she answered softly, "No...not really."

Again there was silence until Richard asked, "Do you go out?"

"Oh, occasionally, but just to dinner or something," she answered.

"Well, I mean—," he started.

"Why don't we skip this," she said deeply. Then turning toward him, she said, "I'm with you and I want to be with you. Let's leave everybody else out."

Again one could hear the gentle dreariness of the rain.

"Why do you like *me?*" he asked, feeling the question inane.

"I liked you from the moment I saw you," she answered, as if asking the question herself. "I don't know—I don't know if women ever know."

"But try," he asked, strangely elated.

"Oh, certainly your body," she answered, tightening her embrace. "And your hair—I'm a real idiot for blond men. And your ... vulnerability. You seem so ... trusting."

"I don't know if I like that or not," he said.

"But I like that. I trust that," she said, kissing him.

"I'll tell you what I like," he said, moving his hand to her buttocks.

"What's that?" she asked playfully, moving her body onto his.

"You probably like a lot of the same things I do," he said, trying to see her face in the darkness.

And the two began moving in harmony.

8

T HE TINY JET sat poised at the end of the runway, its engines whining impatiently. The whole world seemed motionless in the early morning dark, and time seemed to stand still. Richard sat peering out a small window, while Warwick and Sammie leaned back in their seats asleep. To Richard the moment was sad and dreadful, as if all color and life had been drained from his being and he were about to be launched into another, less human dimension.

Suddenly the whine began to rise gradually in pitch and intensity, until it became nearly deafening. And then with a jolt, the craft began rolling down the runway. Almost too quickly its speed began to increase, the whine becoming a scream. And then with a powerful thrust, it lifted itself gracefully off the ground and streaked toward the heavens.

The plane quickly reached low gray clouds and punched into them fearlessly. It then began to jolt and sway as it challenged the powerful forces of the storm. Richard's eyes darted around the interior, first to the cockpit where the pilots calmly played with dials and levers, then to the luxurious leather appointments and costly fittings. He then looked out to the tiny wings, which were barely visible in the swirling miasma, and for a fleeting second he felt as if they were his own.

As soon as the plane broke out of the first layer of clouds, Warwick awoke and stretched. He then nudged Sammie, and they lifted a table from the wall between them and began shuffling cards. Richard felt a wave of humiliation; what to him was awesome and thrilling was to the rich and powerful simply a game room.

"There, you dog!" Warwick shouted, throwing a card on the table. "That's the one you've been waiting for!"

"No, no," Sammie chuckled quietly, stretching his powerful shoulder forward to retrieve the card. "It just adds more trash to the pile. But here, that's the one you've been wet-dreamin' about."

Warwick leaned forward dramatically to peer at the card. A wide grin began spreading across his smooth face, and he began laughing gutturally. "The turkey finally gobbled; the turkey finally gobbled!"

Warwick grabbed a score pad and began writing, while Sammie gathered the cards and shuffled. "You're a real turkey, Sammie. A real turkey. Gobble, gobble, *gobble*."

"I'm going to talk with the pilots," Warwick announced. "Gotta see if they know where we're headed."

As Warwick unbuckled and crouched toward the front, Richard decided he would follow. He had had a glimpse of the myriad instruments and equipment when he entered the plane, but he wanted a closer look. Warwick dropped to his knees behind the cockpit, placing an elbow on either pilot's backrest. Richard crouched just behind him.

"Do those clouds have any rain in 'em?" Warwick asked one of the pilots.

"It sure looks like it," the man answered, turning a dial.

"Which way they headed?" Warwick asked.

"Due east, according to the tower," he answered.

Warwick leaned forward to peer out the window, biting his lower lip vigorously. He then twisted around and said, "You want to see the cockpit? Come on up next to me."

Richard joined him on his knees and began peering in awe at the precision and detail of the panel.

"Where's the Gulf Stream?" Warwick asked the other pilot.

"The Gulf Stream?" the pilot asked. "Well, that's a long way from here. It's an ocean river, you might say, which flows from the Gulf of Mexico all the way to Europe. It's real important to the climate; it carries water from the tropics all the way to Ireland and England. That's why their weather is so moderate."

"What causes it?" Warwick asked softly.

"Oh, let's see," the pilot mused. "I believe it's the rotation of the earth—something like that. The rotation creates a jet stream in the air that moves the water along with it."

"Why has the jet stream moved?" Warwick asked, turning his head to within inches of the pilot.

"Moved?" the pilot asked, turning his head to look

straight at Warwick. "Something like that never moves—it's been there forever."

"What would happen if it did?" Warwick asked, still staring at the man.

"Huh, I don't know," he replied. "It would sure change the weather around."

Warwick continued looking at the side of the pilot's face. Then he slowly turned his head toward Richard and whispered, "We're all sailing in new seas, and even the captains are lost." Richard made no reply, so Warwick asked, "Aren't you afraid?"

"No," Richard answered.

A big grin swept Warwick's face as he leaned forward whispering, "Gobble, gobble, gobble."

It was still raining when the three arrived in New York. A limousine met them at the private terminal and sped them toward the city. Warwick and Sammie drank Bloody Marys and told jokes while Richard perused the passing scene. The rain had turned all the buildings into a dreary monotone, and he wondered why anyone would want to live in such desolation. But he felt warm and secure inside the long Cadillac. He had never been in a limousine before, and he grinned as he rubbed the crushed velvet armrest.

They finally arrived in the financial district and pulled up in front of the Cotton Exchange. Warwick told the driver he could go to lunch, as they would be in the building for several hours. Then the three leaped from the car and raced inside. They walked quickly through the lobby and took an elevator to an upper floor. There they walked down a dimly lighted hallway until they arrived at a half-glass door with W.E. Morgan & Son stenciled in black.

Warwick burst through the door, surprising two older men bent over desks covered with accounting sheets. Warwick ignored them and proceeded through another door into a small, bare private office. He immediately whipped off his jacket and grabbed a short, light cotton smock from a coat rack. "Here, put one of these on," he ordered Richard. As soon as Richard got into the trading jacket, Warwick told the two older men he was going to the trading floor. Sammie asked Warwick how much he wanted on San Diego. "Ten," was the answer. Warwick then retraced his steps to the elevator, Richard hurrying to keep up.

When they arrived at the trading floor, Richard was totally unprepared for what he saw. Inside the high-ceilinged room was a large group of men packed around the perimeter of a circular wooden railing perhaps twelve feet in diameter. They were shouting, sometimes screaming, at each other, flailing their arms and gesturing brutally. The din was so great that Richard couldn't understand a word they were saying.

Warwick proceeded directly toward a row of booths along one side of the room. There he grabbed the elbow of a young man talking vigorously on a telephone. The two talked ear to ear for several seconds until finally they both straightened and nodded. Warwick then proceeded toward the ring and reached through several layers of traders to tap another young man on the shoulder. As if touched by the Master, the young man immediately became normal and struggled to the edge of the crowd. There he and Warwick conversed ear to ear for a number of minutes, the young man nodding periodically. Eventually Warwick raised his head, slapped his colleague on the back and turned. The young man quickly returned to his madness.

Warwick walked by Richard, motioning for him to follow. They left the roar of the room and returned to the elevator. Warwick was silent during the ride and the walk back to the office. Once inside, he marched to the private room, motioning Sammie away from the chair behind the desk. Once seated he leaned back and closed his eyes. He sat motionless for several minutes. Sammie left the room, closing the door behind him.

"You all right?" Richard finally asked.

"Yeah," Warwick sighed, sitting up in his chair. "At times like this I get too high. I have to calm myself down."

"Well, what's happening?" Richard asked.

"It came to me out on the boat," he answered to the desk. "You could see from the studies we were in for a wet fall, and it's going to get wetter. I'm putting on a pretty big bet they won't get the crop in, or not much of it. I'm buying as many as two thousand December contracts— we've already got twelve hundred done."

"How much is a contract?" Richard asked.

"Fifty thousand pounds," he answered.

Richard was stunned. There wasn't much cotton grown in east Tennessee, but he knew a huge bale was less than five hundred pounds. And there were marginal farmers who raised whole families on two or three a year.

"But it's not this year's crop that's important," Warwick continued. "If that jet stream's really moved, and my meteorologists say it has, there's going to be some really screwy weather next spring—late rains, flooding. It's next year's crop I'm going to buy, with everything I've got. It's selling real cheap—forty-five cents a pound— and it's going to go to a dollar."

A dollar a pound! Richard exclaimed to himself. Only once in history had cotton sold for a dollar a pound, and that was in Liverpool when the Union blockaded the Confederacy. Warwick must be nuts; cotton could never go to a dollar a pound!

"My only problem buying next year's contracts is the liquidity of the market. So what I plan to do is this—if I'm right on this year's crop, I'm going to roll it over into next year's through spreads. Plus I'll get another house or two to start buying deferreds for me—Cahnman Brothers, for instance. They do a lot of deferred hedging for the Europeans. Or maybe use Merrill Lynch; they're always wrong."

The two fell silent, the rain pelting away at the grime on the window. Richard sensed he was in the middle of something momentous, but he didn't understand enough to know what was really happening. All he knew was that there were fifty thousand pounds to a contract, and a fifty-cent price move would be worth twenty-five thousand dollars. And Warwick was buying two thousand contracts, and more. He started to speak when he was interrupted.

"You want in on the action?" Warwick asked casually. "I put Sammie in."

"Why . . . well, I don't have the money, War," Richard answered.

"You don't need any money," Warwick said. "The margin's only a few grand on ten contracts, and Empire Trading knows I'm good for it."

"But . . . but, War I don't have the money to *lose*," Richard said.

"You're only going to buy ten new Dec' contracts," War said wearily. "And after you've bought ten contracts, I'm going to buy thousands. Anytime you want out, you just say so. I don't think the price is going to go down much after I start buyin'."

Richard felt ashamed when he realized what Warwick was saying. He was virtually giving him money—for with all that buying, the prices had to go up regardless of other factors. Before he could answer, Warwick picked up the telephone and dialed. After a pause he said, "Mike? War Morgan. How ya doin'? Listen, open an account in the name of Richard Johnson. Then buy ten new Dec' contracts at-the-market-immediate. I'm good for the debit. Okay? Thank you." And he hung up.

Warwick looked at Richard for several seconds, and they both knew that something had changed. Warwick had revealed his most secret plans to Richard, and Richard had allowed his friend to involve him in a highly risky venture. The silence bespoke their understanding.

Warwick then lifted the receiver and dialed another number. After a pause, he said, "Give me Mark Cahnman, please." There was another pause before he greeted his party. "Mark? War Morgan. How ya doin'? That's good. Listen, I need to buy a few new Dec' contracts and I want you to do it for me. I've bought so much Dec' for hedging lately, I'm afraid I'd screw up the market if I did it myself. You mind helping?"

There was a pause while Warwick bit his lip.

"Fine," he continued. "Buy up to five hundred over the next several days. Use your best broker—Lutrell, I guess—and tell him you'll pay extra. Don't tell him it's for me; there's a little thief in everybody, you know. If something unusual comes up, you know how to contact me. Call Jones in my office here if you need any money. I thank you."

Warwick replaced the receiver and immediately picked it up again. He dialed new numbers and waited. "Phillip, this is War. Start buying new Dec' and selling old Dec' spreads for me. Do fifty at a time, unless you get a big offer at a good price. When you've done two hundred, call me."

Warwick replaced the receiver and leaned back in his chair to stretch. "I'll tell you one thing, big boy. Whatever happens between now and next spring, they'll know we're around. Listen, I've got to spend some time on the phone. Why don't you go down to the floor and watch the action. I'll tell Anderson to take care of you."

Richard returned hurriedly to the trading floor. He was anxious to learn more about this bizarre business, especially now that he had a position. At the door a handsome young man met him. "I'm Anderson," he said. "If you have any questions, let me know."

The frantic pace around the ring had subsided—perhaps because traders were at lunch—and now Richard could see what was happening. The process was an auction market where brokers auctioned off the orders to buy or sell at the best price available. It was much like a livestock auction on Saturdays back home. Even at this reduced pace Richard found the action exciting. The men he was watching were trading in millions of dollars' worth of cotton, and even a move of a few tenths of a cent a pound could mean a lot of money won or lost. And Richard was now part of this community; he too was a player. If Warwick was right—and apparently he always was—his contract for December delivery the following year would increase in value, and he would make money on it. How much? he pondered to himself. He thought he'd ask the clerk.

"Well, you're long ten new Dec's," Anderson mused, while watching his multiline telephone. "If it goes up a dime, you'd make about fifty thousand dollars."

Richard was stunned. "Well, what if it goes to a dollar?" he stuttered.

"Oh, shit, it'd be worth a quarter million," he laughed. "But don't go spend it. That's impossible."

Richard was speechless. If Warwick were right, he'd win over two hundred thousand! But if he were even partly right, he'd be rich! His head felt light, and his arms tingled. Just then the tempo in the ring picked up, the shouting growing louder and angrier. Traders and runners began streaming from desks and chairs on the side. Something was happening, but Richard couldn't tell what it was. Then more came pressing in, shoving and elbowing their way toward the center. And the pitch raced higher and higher, and the sounds more chaotic and frantic, the mass swaying and moaning in hysteria. Until finally an order began to emerge, a consensus among the havoc. And they all began screaming the same words over and over again—*Limit bid! Limit bid! Limit bid!*

The hotel suite was splendid—four bedrooms, a kitchen, even a sauna. And the view of the city was breathtaking, the clouds and mist teasing the multitude of lights to dance and flicker. Warwick lay stretched out on one of the long sofas, giving detailed instructions to room service over the telephone. Sammie played solitaire on the enormous glass and teak coffee table. Richard sat uncomfortably in the soft armchair, unable to acclimate to the luxurious surroundings and unwilling to pretend he felt at ease with them. He would simply let the others take the lead.

Warwick slammed down the telephone and picked up

his drink. "Food's on its way," he announced. "Anybody want another drink?"

"No, but I've got a question," Richard asked, boldly stretching out his legs and placing them on the coffee table. "What happened to me today?"

"You got about a cent 'n' a half," Warwick answered, taking a long sip of his drink. "That means you made about seventy-five hundred dollars. Not a bad trade for a lawyer."

"Are you kidding?" Richard asked, breaking into a broad grin. "That's incredible."

"Hell, yeah," Warwick replied, pulling his tie from his neck. "You're going to be a rich man."

Richard was euphoric. He had never had seventy-five hundred dollars at one time in his life. And if he had made that much, Warwick must have made over a hundred times that amount. No wonder he could afford the jet and the fancy service. For a moment he thought of taking his profit and closing the account. But he couldn't do that; it would appear unseemly.

Warwick and Sammie resumed their game of gin, so Richard stood and began to explore the suite. He walked into a bedroom and felt his feet sink into the deep, soft carpet. He wondered how the hotel could keep everything so nice when it was rented out to strangers. Inside the bathroom he found gold-plated fixtures and marble-lined showers. The towels even were monogrammed with the initials of the hotel. He could buy a new car, he told himself; with seventy-five hundred dollars he could buy that new little Porsche. He then heard sounds from the living room. When he returned he saw two liveried waiters setting up service on the dining room table. They had two carts laden with food—giant shrimp in cocktail glasses, caviar, and smoked salmon. And they were setting up chafing dishes to prepare steak *au poivre*. Warwick was directing the operation.

"Decant that wine," he demanded brusquely. "And be sure the *blanc de blanc* is well chilled; I don't like it any way but real *cold*."

Sammie stood to the side, leafing through a book from the floor-to-ceiling shelf behind the sofas. Richard wondered why Sammie was so cool to him. After all, he was dating his sister, and they came from much the same background. But he supposed Sammie was really there to entertain Warwick, to make money gambling with him and placing bets for him. He probably didn't want to mix apples with oranges.

"Find any companionship?" Warwick asked Sammie while tucking a large linen napkin into his open collar.

"Sure did," Sammie answered in singsong. "Be here about eight."

"Come on, Rich," Warwick said, gesturing with a shrimp. "We've got to eat all this."

Richard had never been with a prostitute before, and he said nothing as she walked to the bed and turned on the radio. She was average height with light brown, almost blonde, hair. Her features were pleasant, but something

91

made them less than perfect. Perhaps the cheekbones, which were too large; or the eyes, which were vaguely oriental—Slavic perhaps. She wore a simple blue dress with a thin, white belt.

Richard didn't know what to do. It would be foolish to seduce a whore. But need one be polite, or make small talk? Before he said anything, she rose from the bed and began undressing. As the dress fell to the floor, Richard knew its simplicity had a function—it came off easily. And how much does it cost? he asked himself as he watched her unhook her bra. Her body was that of any other pretty girl; everything was in its proper place—nothing ugly or out of proportion. And he thought of Irene and how exciting her body was to him and how much she was part of the excitement of her body. Surely she could never do this? Why would anyone do this?

The girl walked naked toward him and began unbuttoning his shirt. He simply watched as she undressed him further—even his socks. And his thoughts began to collide as he touched her shoulder and found it soft and smooth—the skin of a stranger, and he hadn't even caught her name. He could do whatever he wanted, he supposed, with the stranger, his object.

He watched her watching him grow and awkwardly placed his arms around her shoulders, still not finding words. And she returned the embrace. But something within him was awry; he felt that this was wrong, and that he didn't want this new world where people were objects, things.

"Let's take a shower," he said.

9

THE LAST TRACES of warmth and growth came and then left the Delta with an ominous brevity. It was no ordinary fall—no brightly colored leaves and pacific blue skies—for it continued to rain day after day under dreary, leaden skies. The usually bright and festive harvest season became soiled with bent, late-blooming flowers and the sound of mud gushing from potholes.

And the cotton stayed in the fields, becoming more and more damaged every day. If the rain would only relent for two weeks—ten days even—there would be time to save the bumper crop. But as each drizzly hour passed, nerves became tighter and spirits more depressed, as everyone from small farmers to huge mill owners began calculating the odds. And their thoughts gave voice every session in the heat and sweat of the Exchange: *"Limit bid! Limit bid!"*

But to some the events were fabulous. Richard's account went from seventy-five hundred dollars to twenty thousand, then forty-five and sixty. He even took some money out of the account to buy the sports car—a Fiat convertible—and to send money home. It was four times the money he would make all year as a lawyer, and he would have to look at his account several times a day to remind himself it was true.

The rest of his life, however, was in turmoil. He was finding it more and more difficult to sit for long hours at work. He enjoyed the law itself—solving problems and finding answers—but he found himself frequently wondering where it would lead. Up to that point the law had been an adventure, but now it seemed as if Arnold Player had turned it into just another job, like that of a plumber or bank clerk.

But it was Irene who kept him most disturbed. He was ecstatic when around her—the deep voice, delicate skin, and quick smile. But when they were separated, he would become depressed and desperately lonely. And he found himself dependent upon any clue or hint of her affections—a prolonged look or a flattering word. Several times he started to ask her if she loved him, but he felt that would be unfair, or dangerous.

And it bothered him most that she traveled with Sammie. His was an illegal business. And besides, it took her away from him. It was during one of those weekends that Irwin came home late and was surprised to find Richard still up watching television.

"What the hell you doing here?" he asked, shaking his raincoat.

"Having a party," Richard answered dourly. "The band's taking a break."

"I thought you'd be out with your lady-love," Irwin said, heading toward the refrigerator to retrieve a beer.

Instead of answering, Richard asked, "Why are you here, get turned down?"

94

"Damned right!" Irwin replied, popping the top. "I sat there and bought drinks for this bitch all night, and when I ask if she wanted to come over, she said she's married. I told her that didn't bother me, but she said it would be *immoral.* Well, what's so goddamn *moral* about conning me out of twenty bucks' worth of booze?"

Richard laughed and stood to turn off the television.

"Say," Irwin asked, walking to a chair, "how's it going with the Moody girl?"

"Oh, fine, I guess," Richard replied, unwilling to explain why he was home alone on Saturday night.

"Well, it's none of my business," Irwin said, taking a seat. "But I grew up in this town, and I feel I know a few things you don't."

Richard tensed, fearful of what he would say about Irene. Irwin had always been a bit jealous of Richard's position as a lawyer with the biggest firm in the city, and it seemed to carry over into their social lives. "Go ahead," he sighed.

"Well, that's a pretty fast crowd you're running with," Irwin started. "All those big cotton families are the same; they've always felt they didn't have to live by the same rules as the rest of us. They always had lots of money, travel, sophistication—things like that. They always felt they were a different caste and could do anything they wanted—an arrogant bunch of bastards. They live here and make their money here, but they want to live like they're in Saint-Tropez or somewhere."

"They take a crap every morning just like you and me,"

Richard said wearily, surprised he found most Memphians so provincial after growing up in a small town himself.

"Yeah, but they don't give a damn," Irwin continued, staring at his beer can. "They'll chew you up and spit you out."

Richard didn't reply. He was becoming so angry he was afraid he would say something irreparable.

"And that Sammie character is...is *Mafia* or something," Irwin continued.

"Oh, *hell*," Richard answered in disgust. "Just because he's a gambler doesn't mean he's Mafia."

"All bookies are Mafia, jerk," Irwin argued. "Where do you think they lay off the bets?"

"If it weren't Sammie, it would be somebody else," Richard answered, knowing Irwin was right.

"And Irene is mixed up with it," Irwin said. "She's there for a reason—"

"Shut your goddamn mouth!" Richard interrupted, rising. "You're nothing but a hick like the rest."

Richard couldn't find further words because he didn't know the answers. But he wasn't going to show that. He couldn't. The two remained in silence, each looking at a different part of the darkened room.

"I suppose I should apologize," Irwin said quietly.

"I'd appreciate it," Richard mumbled.

"Well, I do apologize," Irwin said, "but I wish you'd be careful—"

"Please *quit* all that," Richard interrupted again. "That's insulting too."

"Okay," Irwin conceded. "It's late. I'm going to hit the sack."

"Here's your mail," Martha said, placing several letters and packages on Richard's desk.

"Thank you," he replied, looking up from his tax service. "Have you gotten to that Osgood contract yet?"

"Yeah, but it's not finished," she answered, straightening some of the documents on his desk. "My machine's on the blink, and I'm using Patte's."

"How have you been lately?" he asked, putting the book to one side.

"Oh, fine," she sighed. "With all this rain there hasn't been a whole lot going on. How about you? You've been rather quiet lately. Is anything the matter?"

"Not really," he answered, looking toward the window. "I'm just getting a little bit bored with the work, I guess."

"Everything gets routine after a while," Martha said. "That's what you realize when you get to be my age. Just think, some of these lawyers have been here almost fifty years."

"Sounds about as interesting as a cow-fartin' contest," Richard said.

Martha burst into laughter, covering her mouth and blushing. "That's the funniest thing I've ever heard," she said between gasps. "I might even tell that to my husband."

The two laughed together, until they were interrupted by the telephone. Richard picked up the receiver and heard Arnold's voice.

"Can you step down this way for a minute?" he asked.

"Why, certainly," Richard replied. "Should I bring anything special?"

"No, just want to talk with you," he replied.

Richard hung up the receiver and looked at Martha. "Looks like another judo lesson," he said, twisting his mouth.

"You might prepare yourself for a little chewing out," Martha said discreetly. "He said something to his secretary this morning."

"Oh, great," he mumbled, rising. "I'll let you know what happens."

Richard left the office and walked down the long hall to Arnold's office. He tapped lightly and entered, finding Arnold with his chair turned toward the window and the river. He swiveled around as Richard took a seat.

"What's been bothering you, Rich?" he asked.

The hair on Richard's neck bristled, both from fear and resentment. "I don't know," he answered, hesitant to speak the truth.

"Well, your performance is simply not up to par," Arnold said. "You've been coming in late. You've been getting the work in behind time. The quality of the writing and research isn't what you're capable of doing. You're sullen with the other associates, and you even snapped at one of the partners the other day. That just won't do."

Richard stared at the floor. He knew Arnold was serious, and he knew the wrong answer could get him fired.

"Look, Rich," Arnold said, folding his arms and leaning back. "You're a fine young man, very well trained. But you need to think about whether you want to be a lawyer. If you apply yourself up here for a number of years, you'll do very well. But your attitude has got to improve, there's no two ways about it."

Richard looked up at Arnold, wishing he could tell him about the money he had made trading cotton. But he held back. "I understand," he said. And he stood and left.

Warwick jabbed at the flaming logs with a long iron poker, sending showers of sparks across the hearth. New flames then leaped up to consume the new log he placed on the top. "You think he'd really fire ya?" he asked, while watching the flames' progress.

"I guess so," Richard answered with resignation.

"Look at it this way," Warwick said, returning to his chair. "You're young and well prepared, and you're gonna make some nice money in the market. Who needs those bastards?"

"Heck, I've already made some nice money," Richard replied, lifting his glass.

"Yeah, but some *real* money," Warwick said, still watching the fire. "We really got the shorts on the run, especially the exporters. Nobody knows it yet, but they've made some big commitments to the Red Chinese. When they start hedging that stuff, they'll really blow the roof off."

"How do you know that?" Richard asked, discouraged that there was still so much he didn't know about the business.

"We keep an office in Hong Kong," he answered. "It doesn't do a whole lot. It's just there to keep tabs on what everybody else is doing. Ever been to Hong Kong? Nice place."

The way the question was asked, Warwick knew he'd never been to Hong Kong, so Richard didn't feel the need to answer.

"I bought you ten more contracts," Warwick said matter-of-factly.

"Damn," Richard said. "That's got me up to forty."

"You ought to buy ten every five-cent move," Warwick said. "Always add to a winner."

"You're the boss," Richard said, knowing the profits were approaching a hundred thousand dollars.

"Listen," Warwick finally said, turning in his seat. "Why don't you quit wasting your time with that bunch of fat asses and come work with me."

"Hell," Richard answered in genuine surprise, "you don't need a full-time lawyer."

"Well, I could sure use one," Warwick answered,

standing to return to the fire. "Plus I need someone to help me with the deals I'm getting into. I've got a bundle of cash to invest. It'll be fun."

"It does sound fun," Richard answered pensively. "I'd never thought about being anything but a lawyer. Can you give me a little time?"

"Sure," Warwick answered quickly, poking the fire again and again. "Take your time."

I'll tell you what we can do this weekend," Richard said, loading the last dish into the ancient dishwasher.

"What's that?" Irene asked, as she scrubbed away at the cracked counter with a dishrag.

"I want to go to the zoo," he said ponderously. "I hear it's a great one."

"I'd like to do that," she said, surveying her work. "I haven't been to a zoo in a long time."

"I jog around there," he said, straightening up. "And it looks really neat."

Irene spread the dishrag along the edge of the counter and then turned and leaned against it with her arms folded. Richard noticed her shiny, silken hair hanging down like a stream, dividing as it hit her shoulders.

"That was really good," Richard said, leaning over and kissing her lightly on her neck. The hair and skin were fragrant. "Listen, why don't you move over here?"

"Oh, I don't think that would be right," she answered, turning away.

"Well, I don't like you living over there," he argued.

"Why not?" she asked, a touch of anxiety in her voice.

"I just don't like it," he answered forcefully.

"Look," she replied, her voice choking suddenly. "Sammie's all I've got. There's nobody else. Our father died shortly after I was born and mom died when I was in college. I've never been close to my stepfather. He's all I've got—all I've ever had. And he's taken care of me. I was always his little sister. And I'm not going to leave him right now. He's . . . he's all I've got." She took her apron from the counter to wipe her eyes.

Richard sat on the edge of the sofa, holding the receiver with his right hand and twisting the cord nervously with his left. "Well, mom, this is the way I look at it," he said. "If there's more money and opportunity in business, then why not take it? I can always go back to the law. It's not like you lose it."

He paused, then resumed. "No, no, I left everything fine, at least I think I did. Mr. Player was a little surprised; in fact, he didn't say anything at first, but I don't think he was offended. He even told me that if everything didn't work out, I should come back and talk with him. He was pretty nice about it."

"That's right—twenty-five thousand a year, plus a cut on the deals we get into," he replied. "And I know the guy. He's got a lot of capital. Why, look at what he's done with my cotton account."

"It's not *gambling*, mom," he insisted. "It's speculation, and there's a big difference. First, you're assuming a risk, not creating one. Second, this guy's one of the insiders, one of the biggest in the world. He knows what's happening, the direction of the market. Besides, I can always get out before I lose all the money. It's really not that risky."

"Okay," he continued after a pause, "I'll send the tuition straight to the university. What should I do with the two hundred each month?"

"Okay," he answered. "I'll send that directly to her. Sure you don't need some? There's plenty."

And then he seemed to twist the cord a bit harder. "But, mom, I still *am* a lawyer, and I always will be. You don't have to go to some stupid office every day, and work for *nothing*, to be a lawyer. A lot of lawyers get into business and do very well. I'm sure dad would agree."

"Okay," he said with relief. "Give everybody my love. I love you too. Okay. Oh, by the way, I've met a new girl—a real looker too. Yeah, real nice. From Alabama. I'll bring her home some weekend. Yeah, you'll really like her."

"Okay. Bye-bye."

10

THE RAINS STOPPED for over a week in December, and the drenched earth responded to the sun. The air turned cool and clear, and cloudless sunsets spread pink and golden rays through the bare trees and wistful trails of smoke from burning leaves. Neighbors lingered longer than usual after dusk, sending out low chatter and unexpected bursts of laughter. Lovers strolled silently through the parks and along solitary country lanes.

Some of the cotton was picked, angry machines churning even through the night to gather what was left. But everyone knew that the perfect flower—the long, seamless, virgin fiber—was lost, leaving only the soiled and the worthless. For the farmers it was a very bad year, but they and their forebears had survived bad crops before. To many, the events were providential—and indeed contained a promise—for now He owed them one in the coming season. To them it was simply another "Chevrolet year" in the Delta.

But not so for the others. Hopes that had risen with news that the weather had lifted were quickly quashed as prices rose higher and higher. Mills ran clamoring to their servants in Congress to demand an embargo. Labor unions joined in, fearing the higher prices would throw their members out of work. And the speculator—he who had no friends—became either rich or poor. Warwick, as well as those around him, was becoming very, very rich.

But while some were licking their wounds, and others celebrating their good fortune, Warwick continued buying futures contracts for the following year. For him the present season's events were simply the prelude to the thundering catastrophe to come. For he believed the rains would return, that God wouldn't fulfill His promise to the faithful in Mississippi. The South would flood in the spring, and it would destroy the cotton industry. It would be a cataclysm worse than the Civil War. It would be total ruin—annihilation.

The spirits around Warwick's estate were high, and he became lavish in his generosity. Irene was given a new car. Richard received expensive clothing from Brooks Brothers and Abercrombie's. Sammie was given a Tennessee walking horse and an antique cello. Warwick bought nothing for himself.

The richest reward for Richard, however, was having succeeded on his own after departing the law firm. It gave him a sense of peace and satisfaction, and he felt a closer kinship with those ancestors who had bravely traversed the mountain wilderness to settle the misty valleys of Appalachia. He had drunk deeply from their cup of independence, and he knew there was no turning back.

There was also no turning back in his feeling for Irene. Her mystery seemed to be the very source of his passion for her. The more silent and secretive she became, the greater grew his desire to possess her, to penetrate her

105

being. But instead of forcing himself upon her, he found himself protecting the mystery and nurturing its power over him, perversely postponing the intimacies and dazzling explosions of sensation.

Warwick's lifestyle began to change. He turned over more and more responsibility to Richard, who found himself busier every day talking with mill owners and factors and employees at the Memphis offices on Front Street. Warwick remained at home most of the time, drinking more and oftentimes not dressing until afternoon, endlessly absorbed with his strategies for the coming campaign. He refused all calls except from Richard or from only the closest associates at the Cotton Exchange. He decided to take delivery of a thousand December futures contracts; he wanted the actual commodity just in the event there were massive defaults and the Exchange collapsed. But he began exercising vigorously, swimming for hours in his heated pool and lifting weights to strengthen his dark, lean body. One day he called Richard to tell him he would pick him up in the Landrover to go to the University Club to play racquet ball. On the way to the game, it began to rain.

"Pour, you son-of-a-bitch!" he shouted gleefully toward the sky. "Pour your guts out!"

"You may like the rain," Richard said, throwing his briefcase over the seat. "But the fellows down at the plantation are having a helluva time. I still think we should have paid them some kind of bonus."

"Screw 'em," Warwick sneered. "When they have a good crop, they want all the credit, but when they have a bad one, they blame it on the weather. I'll be damned glad to get rid of those crybabies."

"What do you mean 'get rid'?" Richard asked.

"Well, I'm going to retire one of these days," Warwick replied quietly.

"Retire?" Richard asked in amazement. "I can't ever see you *retired*."

"Well, get out of the business," Warwick replied vacantly. "Get away from all this tension, be able to relax."

Richard was surprised. It was the first time he had heard Warwick admit that the tensions of the business bothered him. He had always appeared so invulnerable to the pressures felt by ordinary men.

"What in the world would you do?" Richard asked, looking at Warwick's face and seeing no evidence of stress.

"I don't know," he answered. "I'd sure spend a lot of time in a place where it doesn't rain!" They both laughed, and he continued. "There are a lot of interests I'd like to pursue—my stamp collection, fishing—you know, things like that."

"Ever thought about getting married?" Richard asked.

"Shit, no," Warwick replied. "Why buy what you can rent at half the price."

Richard paused after the reply, but then he asked, "What's holding you back? Why don't you retire now?"

"Because I haven't finished," he answered slowly. "I haven't done it yet. I haven't ruined 'em. I haven't seen the blood running."

"Who's that?" Richard asked.

"Listen, the big problem is security," Warwick said. "I want to find some way where the assets are completely safe—you know, the ultimate haven. I haven't figured that out yet."

"Buy government bonds," Richard answered, laughing at the prospect of Warwick buying so conservative an investment.

"Too risky," he replied. "One of these days, they won't be able to give those turds away. Besides, it's *those* folks I'm trying to get away from!"

"Try gold," Richard suggested.

"Yeah, gold, silver, currencies—art, maybe," he mused. "The big deal is the secrecy—something you can't have in the U.S.—and being an American is a pretty good deal right now."

"Well, accumulate some cash—say, in Las Vegas—and just walk it out," Richard blurted.

"Naw, too risky again," Warwick answered, opening the door. "I'll think of something."

The two dashed through the rain and into the building. They dressed in silence, as Richard wondered what had prompted him to suggest smuggling the money out illegally. As soon as they finished, they descended the spiral staircase and entered the small white court.

Richard won the toss for service, so crouched low

against the red service line and whacked the ball against the front wall. Warwick returned it skillfully along the backhand wall. Richard dove toward the ball, passing Warwick with a powerful flick of his wrist. Richard served again and won the next three points. He lost the fourth and handed Warwick the ball. As the game progressed, he again thought of what he had done—counseled a friend to break the law. But he hadn't done it as a lawyer; he had simply advised a friend. The game remained tight, the service passing every one or two points. The room heated up, and both players began to sweat profusely. That was the part Richard liked the most—the close competition and the sensation of accumulated waste pouring from one's pores. Finally, with the score twenty to eighteen, Richard whipped a low, fast ball to the forehand corner, where it dropped and died.

"Nice game, asshole," Warwick sighed, letting his tall frame slide down the wall. "Let's take a breather."

Richard slid down the opposite wall, exhilarated by having beaten Warwick. But he couldn't forget his advice and whether it was wrong. Perhaps that's what one must do when operating in the big leagues, he told himself. Maybe that's the only way life works when it gets so complicated. He himself now had over two hundred thousand in the account, and he too should begin to worry about taxes and security.

Richard looked at Warwick, whose head hung low between his legs. "You okay?" he asked between breaths.

Warwick simply nodded, his breathing becoming less labored. "I just wish it was all over," he said. "The waitin' is really gettin' to me."

Again Richard was surprised—and flattered— to hear Warwick speak of his anxieties. "Take your profits now," he said again. "Winning isn't everything."

"That's where you're wrong," Warwick replied, raising his sweat-soaked face. "That *is* the profit. That's what the whole thing's about. What the hell is a few million dollars; a lot of nobodies got that. It's the winning that counts; my grandfather always taught me that. It's the winning, against everybody else in the world. Watching them suffer—knowing you've won. And I'm going to show him I can do it, better than he ever did. See, I've got to beat him too."

The two stared at each other, each too exhausted to make further sound. Finally, Warwick said, "Come on, turkey, I've got a lesson to teach you. Get off your ass."

And once again they locked into their lonely battle, each pushing and straining himself to the limit. He's right, Richard told himself, as Warwick lobbed a fast one over his left shoulder. Winning is the game; that's what the whole world wants. Winning at business—at sex. It's being the best, the first. "There!" he shouted, sending a screamer past Warwick's feet. "Eat that one!"

The wind moved cruelly through the branches of the defenseless trees, pushed, it seemed, by the dark, ominous clouds racing low overhead. The temperature was dropping, and Irene's perfect skin was becoming raw and puffy.

"You want to go to the aquarium?" Richard asked with a shiver. "It'll be warm inside."

"I want to see the lions and tigers," she answered, firming her grip around Richard's waist. "It'll just take a minute."

Richard let his arm fall from her shoulder to her waist, and even beneath the heavy coat, he could sense the lovely skin and soft musculature. He leaned his head against hers, giving her a small kiss on the forehead. He craved everything about her and wanted to be with her forever.

"The animals are all inside," he observed, as they rounded the walkway toward the mammal house. "Let's see if the door's open."

They pushed against the door and were suddenly engulfed by moist, pungent air. They both sighed with relief and unbuttoned the tops of their coats.

"Is that a he or a she?" Irene asked, running toward one of the tigers.

"They're just like other animals," Richard answered with a chuckle. "I think that's the mama."

They again locked arm around waist and strolled past the caged animals. An employee was shoving hunks of red meat between the bars toward the leopard.

"Why don't you spend the next week with me?" he asked. "We can do something. Maybe go on a little trip somewhere."

"I can't," she answered, stopping suddenly and dropping her lovely eyes. "I'm . . . I'm going away for a couple of weeks."

"Away?" Richard asked in dismay. "Where to?"

"Down to Alabama," she whispered. "To visit my stepfather."

"Shit!" Richard muttered, already in agony from the absence. "Why?"

"I need to visit him," she answered. "I haven't seen him in a long time."

"I'm sorry, Mr. Farr, but that's how we read the contract," Richard said into the receiver. "I'm sorry this misunderstanding has come up."

Richard paused for a moment, leaning in his high-backed chair and grimacing. "Well, I checked with Mr. Morgan, and he can't recall telling you that. I'm afraid its just a question of poor communication," he replied.

"No, no," he answered after another pause. "I don't think that would do any good. We've pretty well made up our minds on this one. We don't want it."

Richard rubbed his eyes while listening further. "I'm sorry you feel that way, Mr. Farr, but I'll tell him you called." He then said goodbye and hung up.

"Got a little pissed, did he?" Warwick asked, shifting his feet on the top of Richard's desk.

"Well, I really can't blame him," Richard answered. "You did tell him you wanted to buy it. He kept yelling that your father never backed out on a deal."

112

"Screw 'em," Warwick answered, his voice slightly slurred from the drinks at lunch. "My father never had to worry about tax shelters. Those were the good old days."

The telephone rang again, and Richard reached to pick it up. "Hello," he said and then listened for several minutes. He then covered the receiver with his hand and turned to Warwick.

"It's Rice over in Arkansas," he whispered. "He wants to speak with you."

"That's why I hired you," Warwick answered, with a belch.

"Yeah, but he thinks we're nuts buying so much production at these prices," Richard answered. "He wants to hear it from you."

"I'm not here," Warwick yawned.

"He's not here," Richard said into the receiver. "But the plan is still the same—keep on buying the acreage. We want a big part of the new crop. We're getting it hedged in New York. War knows what he's doing."

Richard hung up and sighed. "That's the third field guy who's called this week, War. They think we're crazy, I tell you. We're running up the prices all over, they say."

"They're a bunch of hicks with nothing to show for it," Warwick answered, letting his feet fall to the floor. "That's why they're working for me. Just tell 'em to get their asses back to work. Hired help! Hired help! That's why they're hired help!"

Richard let the remark pass. His account was well over two hundred thousand.

11

A S WINTER SET in, a strange malaise infected those living in the Delta. Christmas was joyous for the children, but for their parents it was a time of recollection and worry. The awful rains continued, week after week, occasionally turning into snow or sleet, but always bringing more and more moisture to the already saturated fields. It was a long time between January and planting time, but if the rains didn't stop, it could result in the unthinkable.

Slowly the great river rose, challenging its embankments like a mighty army. Here and there, in dozens of different places, the levees broke, pouring more and more water onto the rich, soggy earth. And what would happen in April, when the northern snow cover melted, all the way from the Appalachians to the Rockies? Old men strained to remember like winters in the past, while the younger cast about frantically for hope.

And the atmosphere on the futures exchange in New York was equally tense. After the debacle of the fall, most traders and firms were financially injured. Many had had to sell their seats—along with their big townhouses and imported sports cars. And those who survived were wary and exhausted, and thankful the fall was over. Surely life would return to normal; there couldn't be another year like the past one. No, things would return to normal. Time would heal all wounds, they counseled.

Warwick slowly emerged from seclusion. He began rising earlier in the mornings and taking calls. The drinking slowed, and his relations with his employees and friends improved. One sensed he felt the agony of waiting was nearing an end, for soon the effects of the winter rains would begin to be felt in the marketplace. And soon the Weather Service would begin to comment on the strange changes in the flow of the air streams, as had his private meteorologists months before. He was like a Spartan warrior girding his loins for battle, gleefully anticipating what to others was fearsome and odious.

Although Richard was enjoying his work, Irene's absence was enormously painful. Her two-week trip became three and then four. She called from Alabama occasionally, but always remained vague as to when she would return, or why she had left. To combat his terrible loneliness, he plunged more deeply into work, studying at night to try to learn this arcane, yet vastly important, business. On many nights he would fall asleep, alone, with a crop report or export contract or loan compilation analysis on his chest.

One morning very early Warwick telephoned to say they were leaving within an hour for New York. Richard had been expecting the call, for he was slowly beginning to realize that Warwick's fortunes—and his own—were rapidly shifting from the dank soils of Mississippi and

Arkansas to the sullied streets of New York. The trip on the jet was dull. The weather bounced the tiny craft the entire way, while Warwick and Sammie slept or played cards. He found himself amazed how, after five or six trips on the Jetstar, it was becoming just another tool.

Once in the city they were met again by the limousine. This time Richard too drank a Bloody Mary, something he had never done during the day. He tried to make small talk with Sammie, but to no avail. They seemed to have no common ground, no shared experience, and Sammie made him feel juvenile and naive. As soon as the limousine arrived at the Exchange, they rushed upstairs. Warwick seemed to know, as always, exactly what he wanted to do with the measured time allotted him. He changed jackets, barked a few orders to the older men seated in the office, and then proceeded to the trading floor. Richard and Sammie trailed behind.

Few people recognized Warwick as he entered the room, probably because very few had ever actually met him. But as he proceeded toward his firm's desk, first one older trader, then another, turned and paused. He walked up behind the floor manager and slapped him hard on the back. The young man jumped, then extended his hand in glee.

"How ya been?" the manager exclaimed, disconnecting his telephone. "Good to see ya!"

"What's happenin'?" Warwick asked, all business.

"No buyers, War," the young man answered sternly. "They won't sell the shit, but they won't buy it either."

"They won't?" Warwick asked, with an involuntary grin. "I heard a lot of guys went broke."

"It's been rough, War, really rough," the manager answered. "And, of course, a lot of 'em blame it on you."

"Good," he answered plainly. "It's going to get a lot rougher. Give me some trading cards."

The manager handed Warwick a stack of cards and a pencil. Warwick took them and turned toward the ring. As he approached, a number of members nudged each other, word having spread that Warwick was on the floor. Just as he reached the ring, a young trader turned, and seeing a new face, yelled, "Sell Dec' even! Sell Dec' even!" Warwick looked at the young trader, his eyes those of a seasoned hawk. The other traders—those who had known his father and grandfather—turned and shook their heads with wry smiles. It was going to be an act of nature, the strong eating the weak and innocent.

But instead, Warwick turned and looked at the other members, men who knew who he was, his heritage, his forebears. And his eyes relaxed, as if it were a home-coming—after almost a hundred years of family involvement on the Exchange. And the others too seemed to feel relief, to feel they were in the presence of a known factor, an old adversary.

So it didn't surprise them when Warwick turned to the young trader and said, "I don't think you want to do that."

"What do you mean?" the young man asked, looking

117

from side to side. "I'm making a market! What do you want to do?"

"I want to buy Dec'," Warwick answered, every veteran within hearing distance feeling a chill.

"Fine. I'll sell you two at even," the young man answered.

"I want to buy a hundred," Warwick replied, his eyes becoming glazed, as if they were scanning the entire room.

"I can't do that," the young man said in confusion, wondering who this fellow his own age was.

"Then get out," Warwick answered viciously, again staring at the young man.

"I have a right to be here," he answered petulantly.

"Fine," Warwick answered. "I'll pay the *limit* for a hundred Dec'."

"With that two men grabbed the kid and dragged him to the side. A small Exchange official stepped forward and announced, "Now listen here, Morgan, we're going to have an orderly market, none of this jamming stuff."

"I'm not jamming a goddamn thing!" Warwick answered angrily. "I bid the limit, and I'll pay it. You want any?"

"But you're running through orders," the man argued, looking up at Warwick's glare.

"I'll buy everything they've got," Warwick answered, turning. "Where are they? Where are the orders? I'll pay the limit!"

As if shaken from somnambulism, the brokers began shuffling through great wads of paper and pulling out the sell orders.

"I'm still not going to tolerate disorderly markets," the official continued.

"Shut up," Warwick mumbled, busily writing down what he was buying. "What could be more orderly than this."

When he finished with the brokers, he turned to the others who had gathered in a large crowd. "All right, I'll pay the *limit* for December. I'll pay *limit for a thousand Dec'!*"

No one said a word. Rich traders—owners of large firms—stood by like schoolboys, waiting for someone to act. Warwick surveyed the crowd, his jaw set. Finally he turned and pushed his way out of the crowd. He threw his cards at the manager at the desk and left the room. Richard and Sammie hurried after him, but not before they heard from the ring: "Limit for Oc'! Limit for Dec'!" Then louder, ever louder, the familiar anthem: *"Limit bid! Limit bid! Limit bid!"*

When Richard returned to the office, he found a sturdy-looking white-haired man patiently waiting for him. The stranger introduced himself as McDonald from Empire Trading and asked if he could speak with him privately. Richard was a little annoyed, but ushered the man into a small office next to Warwick's.

McDonald refused a seat and said, "I'll just be a minute, Mr. Johnson, but I wanted to remind you that you're long over a hundred contracts."

"I know that," Richard answered. "There's more than two hundred thousand in the account. That should be enough to handle margin."

"Oh, yes," McDonald answered, his reddish face forcing a smile. "But I must remind you that if the market should turn, we won't allow any debits."

"What's the big problem?" Richard asked with irritation. "It's been very profitable; besides, it has Morgan's guarantee on it."

"Yes, I know," the old man sighed. "But I've seen this market do some crazy things in my days."

"Look, if you want me to change clearinghouses, I'll be glad to," Richard blurted. "I've paid a lot of commissions!"

"No, no," McDonald answered. "But we would like to have a financial statement."

"Well, you aren't going to *get* one!" Richard shouted. "You're dealing with a gentleman—take it or leave it."

The old man paused and looked at Richard with eyes that revealed nothing. "Well, that'll be all right for now, I guess. But, listen, young man, try to be careful. I've seen 'em take some pretty smart boys out of here feet first."

"You let me worry about that," Richard answered, chafing under the lecture. "How much money you made around here?"

120

"You're a nice boy, Johnson," McDonald said. "I can tell you were brought up right. I hope you'll be careful."

The two lay naked on the sofa, wrapped in a soft, thick blanket. The logs crackled in the huge fireplace, occasionally shifting and breathing, the fire throwing nervous rays of light around the huge, darkened room. The only other sound was that of the distant bitter winds outside the French doors.

"I was worried about you," Richard said softly.

Irene replied with a murmur and nestled her head against Richard's chest.

"What was the matter?" he asked.

"Oh... female trouble," she answered.

"Serious?" he asked.

"Not really," she answered.

"I was wondering whether you'd come back," he said.

"Why?" she asked.

"Because you seemed so distant," he answered.

"Well, I... didn't feel good," she pleaded softly.

"Why didn't you tell me?" he asked.

"Oh, it's all so... unattractive," she answered.

"You're always attractive to me," he said, kissing her on the top of her head.

There was a pause before she rolled over and kissed his chest. He wanted to say he loved her.

"Do you love me?" he asked.

He could feel her head move.

"I don't want you ever to leave again," he said.

She paused again, and then she slowly turned and climbed on top of his body.

The living room in the old house hadn't changed, except for the new television Richard had sent for Christmas. The gas heater still stood in front of the bricked-up fireplace. The ancient horsehair couch, its arms bedecked with doilies, sat flanked by its companion chair and the padded rocker. The small photograph of FDR stared out from its place near the large color reproduction of the Last Supper.

But it was the smell which whisked Richard back to his childhood—that sweet mixture of dust and hickory smoke and a thousand cookings. He could almost see his father now—asleep beside the old standup radio, his sweat-stained collar open beneath his large, bristly jaw. He used to be slightly ashamed of all this, but now he was accepting of it, if not proud. It was all hard and honest and real. He knew where everything—and everyone—was. And that was comforting in his world of things so transient and new.

"I thought you were going to bring your girl with you," his mother shouted from the kitchen.

"She couldn't come," Richard answered, his stomach full of chicken and cornbread. "She was busy this weekend."

"Did you bring a picture?" she asked.

"Why, no, I didn't," Richard answered, a little ashamed he hadn't thought to do so.

His mother entered the room, wiping her hands on an apron. She was a tall woman with graying, reddish hair. She had many of Richard's features, but age and work had made her skin rough and her hands and ankles large. She stood ramrod straight and moved with a determined poise.

"Well, I'm disappointed," she said in her country twang. "You've spoken so much about her."

"I'll bring her next time," Richard mumbled, stretching his legs out in front of him.

"Have you started drinking?" his mother asked quietly, yet sternly, her eyes watching her hands straighten out her skirt. "I know that's not a fair question," she continued, "but I've heard how those people down in Memphis like to live."

"Yeah, I take a drink," Richard answered nervously.

"Do you think you have to?" she asked, moving to the rocker.

"Hey, mom, I'm a big boy now," he laughed. "I can take care of myself. Don't you worry."

"Well, I remember what your father used to say," she said, looking at him. "Life's too wonderful to throw away on a five-dollar bottle of whiskey. It's never done anybody in the world one bit of good, and it's done lots of harm. You can see it with folks right here in this county."

Richard's cheeks burned, and his neck felt huge. Everything she said was certainly true, but he had the right to lead his own life. And suppose she knew about the girls, and the things he did with them. And the business he was in. And Sammie. At least he didn't smoke.

"Just promise me you'll fight it," she said, her voice moving higher and higher.

"Oh, mom," Richard answered, standing involuntarily. "I don't really *drink*."

"That's what I've heard a lot of them say in testimony," she answered. "They say it all starts with one drink."

"Well, I promise I won't, mom," he said, regaining his seat. "I promise I won't."

"What church you going to?" she asked, lifting her head.

"Oh, I've tried several of them," Richard answered, wondering what she would say if she knew the truth.

"They're Baptist, aren't they?" she asked, looking at him.

"Oh, I tried a Methodist one Sunday. I met some nice people who go there," he continued to lie. "And I tried a Presbyterian once."

"Well, you stick with the Baptists, son," she counseled. "The Baptists never waver. What church is your girl?"

"She's Baptist," Richard answered. "So's her family."

"I wish my life were like *that*." Warwick mused, the strains of a Mozart clarinet concerto pouring from the car speaker.

"How's that?" Richard answered, himself lost in the landscape.

"It's perfect," Warwick answered distantly, his eyes wide and without focus. "Every note is what it ought to be; there's no flaw. In two hundred years they've never found

124

a flaw. And every time it's performed, it's perfect. Unchangeable."

"I see what you mean," Richard answered, scanning the lifeless countryside.

Jason slowed the car to turn, and Richard saw a lonely wooden shack set back from the corner. A thin trail of smoke crept from its stone chimney, which jarred his memory and took him back to his earliest recollections. His parents lived in a house much like that when his older sister was born. There was no central heat, or electricity, or plumbing. His mother cooked in a big open fireplace, which was their only source of warmth. And he remembered lying snug in bed on the cold mornings, crawling out only after hearing the crackle of new logs placed on the still smoldering fire. He remembered cracking the ice in the basin of the old commode to wash his face and sitting on the chilly metal chamber pot kept for the children. And then the long hot afternoon sitting on the porch listening to his mother moan and grunt with the doctor, wondering if she were sick and dreading that she might be dying, being reassured only by the lively gossip of the neighbor ladies who had come with food. He remembered walking into the new house, which wasn't really new, but had a bathroom inside and a gas heater in the living room and electric lights that turned on and off by simply pulling a string. There was nothing wrong with all that, until he went off to school and met kids whose families rode in automobiles, instead of trucks or wagons,

125

and had carpets and televisions and servants. He started to ask Jason to stop the Cadillac and turn back toward the cabin. But instead, he shuddered.

12

IN THE MIDDLE of February the rain turned to snow and ice, and most southern communities, unused to such conditions, became prisoners to the elements. And for a while everyone forgot about the cotton industry. More important was clearing the driveway or restoring power or getting the kids to school.

But on the Cotton Exchange the players couldn't forget. The contractual obligations remained in place, the wheel stood poised. Fear of natural cataclysm was now pandemic, and prices reached their highest levels since the 1860s. But, still, the mills were loath to pay seventy-five cents a pound—that would surely price their products out of the market. But what would happen if they had to pay eighty or ninety, or even a dollar? Almost total paralysis prevailed, as they all waited for the wheel to spin.

Warwick too waited, again lapsing into bouts of drinking to fight insomnia. He knew he had won, but he wanted the spoils; he wanted the panic to begin, as an end to his own suffering. At the Exchange he would stop traders and berate them, calling them turkeys and cowards for not having the courage to move ahead. His floor privileges were finally revoked, and he was asked not to return in person. So he retreated to the mansion in Memphis, holed up with his liquor and ticker tape and

Sammie. But he knew he would return some day, and they would grovelingly hand him the key.

Richard had no time for such thoughts, for he was too busy running the firm. The vast amounts of profit from the fall had to be invested and diligently watched. He had to hire more staff and travel throughout the cotton belt to see how Warwick's empire was performing. Warwick increased his salary to fifty thousand dollars and gave him percentages of most of the deals. He was often tired, but otherwise happier than he had been in his life. Irene was with him almost constantly, and their feelings for each other were growing stronger.

Toward the end of February, prices on the Exchange began to slip. Word was out that it was a technical adjustment, or perhaps profit-taking. Warwick angrily sent word that he hadn't sold a single contract, and anyone who did was doomed. The erosion was tiny, but it was enough to send him privately into paroxysms of rage and bouts of drinking. Richard would say nothing during these episodes; Warwick had always been right, and it was his job to keep the profits coming.

On a Saturday morning after one of those late-night drinking bouts Richard walked into the kitchen to find Irwin cooking at the stove.

"Want some grub?" Irwin asked. "You look like you need it."

"Yeah, thanks," Richard mumbled, rubbing his head. "Throw a couple of eggs on, if you don't mind."

"What's happening to that damned cotton market?" Irwin asked, cracking an egg.

"What do you mean?" Richard asked with a yawn.

"That stuff's fallen four or five cents in the last week," Irwin answered, cracking the other egg. "Is the big blow over?"

"I don't think so," Richard replied, looking for the sports section. "I haven't been keeping up with it, but nothing major's in the wind."

"Hell, that's a lot of money," Irwin said. "I can remember when cotton didn't move a nickle all year."

"It's going to a dollar," Richard mumbled. "There's big flooding coming this spring."

"That guy in the *Commercial* says it's going to drop thirty-five cents," Irwin said.

"That's bullshit," Richard replied. "Why's he working for a newspaper?"

"All this talk about an oil embargo, he says," Irwin said, lifting the eggs from the skillet. "It's going to create a recession."

"Mills got to run on something," Richard answered. "Ladies got to have dresses."

"It ought to be interesting," Irwin said, delivering the plates to the table. "Bon appetit!"

It wasn't until later that the conversation with Irwin bothered Richard. He was on his way to the office when it occurred to him that a five-cent move would cost him many thousands of dollars. Cotton had never gone down since he opened his account, and it made him uneasy to think he had given back part of his profit. He parked the car directly in front of the old building on Front Street and used his key to open the street door. Once inside he climbed the slanting stairs two at a time to the second floor. He was surprised to find the inner door unlocked.

The office interior betrayed the shabby, fragile appearance from the street. There were thick carpets on the floor and expensive paintings and photographs on the walls. The slick, elegant surroundings could have been anywhere—New York, London, Zurich. He walked down the long hallway, seeing a light in Warwick's private office. When he reached the door, he saw Warwick bent over a safe in a cabinet behind his desk.

"Whatcha doin?" Richard asked with a grin.

"God*damn!*" Warwick gasped, wheeling to reach for a revolver on top of the desk.

"Hold it, War!" Richard shouted in shock. "It's only *me!*"

Warwick stared with eyes wide, the hand with the revolver trembling. "What the hell are you doing here?" he whispered in confusion.

"I work here, remember?" Richard answered, his palms extended. "I just came down to clean up my desk."

"Why are you in this office?" Warwick asked, his eyes moving from side to side. "Why are you in this *office?*"

"War, it's me, it's Rich," he answered. "I'm supposed to be here. I'm your—partner."

Warwick's face suddenly relaxed, the hand replacing

the revolver on the desk. He let his head drop and shoulders fall. "Don't ever come in this office," he said softly. "This is my office—*my office.*"

"Okay, okay," Richard answered, backing toward the door. "There's nothing wrong. Everything's all right. Just relax—"

"Please don't ever come in this office. This is *my* office," Warwick repeated.

"I understand," Richard answered, bewildered by the revolver and the strange behavior. "Don't worry, I won't."

"I'm just checking some documents," Warwick said, turning toward the safe. "You didn't see a thing, you understand?"

"I didn't see a thing," Richard assured him, noticing for the first time the stubbled beard and darkened eyes. "Say, are you all right?"

"Yeah, I'm all right," Warwick answered breathlessly. "I just need a vacation—go somewhere."

"Everybody's been telling you that," Richard said with a laugh. "You're certainly not your old self these days. Where you want to go?"

"I want to go skiing," he answered, his eyes still darting around the room. "Yeah, skiing. Colorado—no, Europe. France, maybe—no Switzerland—that's it—Switzerland. We're all going to Switzerland."

"Listen, War, something's the matter with you," Richard said, stepping forward. "You're not acting right—I mean it."

"Nothing skiing won't cure," Warwick answered, looking again toward the safe. "You just gave me a scare. Thought it was a couple of thugs or something. I want to leave right now. I can call the travel agent and get us out of here this afternoon."

"Whoa!" Richard shouted with a grin. "I can't leave right now. I've got a meeting with the banks Monday morning and with the compress boys from Texas in the afternoon."

"Go to the bank meeting," Warwick said, looking at Richard for the first time. "Postpone the Texas thing till after we get back."

"Okay," Richard laughed, hoping it would calm Warwick. "But they're going to be pissed; in fact, they wanted the meeting with you."

"Just tell 'em I'll be at the meeting when we get back," he answered. "Tell 'em we've gone to New York. Don't mention the skiing thing—they'll think we're screwin' off."

"Sounds fine," Richard answered cheerfully. "You book the reservations, and I'll be there."

Warwick nodded and turned his gaze toward the top of the desk. After a moment Richard shrugged and left the room. Proceeding down the hall, he felt a mixture of uneasiness and joy. He was going skiing in Europe, a world he'd always dreamed of seeing. Yet he also felt he'd been insulted; his friend had been so defensive, so exclusive. Was this just further indication of his being "hired help"? But of course not. Warwick wanted to take him to Switzerland. That meant he was still part of the inner circle. And, after all, who else was included? Probably Sammie and surely Irene, and they weren't any closer than—perhaps not so close as—he was. This too would be explained, Richard reasoned, as he took a seat at his paper-laden desk. Warwick's a strange man, but he always returns to the norm. Just give him time. He's in control.

Richard thumbed through the pile of new mail placed on top of the heap and came across his statement from Empire Trading. He opened it casually and looked at the balance in his account. A cold sensation swept through his body as he saw the numbers. He had lost fifty thousand dollars since he last looked at the sheets. He hadn't noticed that Warwick had continued to buy more contracts for him—at ever and ever higher levels—and now even a small drop in value was very costly. He sat staring at the paper for several minutes, his mind reeling. But then he reminded himself that business wasn't all profit; there must be a few losses occasionally. After all, he still had over two hundred thousand in the account, more than he had ever had in his life. And it would be going higher soon. It always did. And he felt wiser. He had learned something new in this strange world of speculation.

Their union had been exquisite, not only in its finely wrought and intense pleasure, but also in the wondrous relief each felt in sharing the same personality. And they lay together silently in the aftermath, feeling the meld slowly abate, along with the exhaustion and tingling.

Neither moved until the front door slammed, a signal that Irwin had returned to go to sleep. Irene stirred and slowly rose to sit on the side of the bed.

"Whatcha doin'?" Richard asked hoarsely.

"I don't want to be here all night," she whispered.

"Why not?" he asked, rolling to his side.

"I...just...don't want to," she answered. "I don't know what Irwin would think."

"Oh, hell, he's seen you here before," Richard answered, his hand finding her back in the darkness.

"Yes, but never at breakfast," she argued in her smooth, deep voice.

"Why do you worry about that?" Richard asked, rising to sit on the side of the bed. "Irwin's just like us. He's a good guy."

"Yeah, but it...looks bad," she said with a shiver. "I don't want him to tell people I'm living over here."

Memories of Irwin's earlier comments returned, and how wrong they had been. It made him happy they were leaving Memphis for a vacation, going to places where people weren't so narrow and bitter. He suddenly remembered he hadn't bought any ski clothes.

"Listen, you've got to go with me to buy ski clothes tomorrow," he said excitedly.

"Tomorrow's Sunday, darlin'," she answered, with another shiver. "I don't think any of the nice stores will be open."

"Where should we look?" he asked, jumping up. "I want to get some really sexy ski pants."

"You'll be lucky to find anything like that around here," she laughed, standing and finding his shoulder. "Why don't you wait till we get to Switzerland; they'll have lots of the latest things."

"Where are you going to get yours?" he asked, bussing her cheek and neck.

"I . . . I'm not too sure I'm going," she answered.

Richard froze in disbelief. "Bull*shit*," he said, his eyes searching for hers in the dark. "Of course you're going."

"But I've never skied before," she mumbled. "Besides, I don't like long plane rides."

"Don't you worry about a thing, Pumpkin," Richard purred, pushing her backward toward the bed. "Ol' Rich'll take care of everything. Skiing's easy. I learned the first time, and it's even easier for girls. It's more damned fun, all that snow and mountains and beautiful air. And feeling the wind rush by as you slip down those runs. But don't worry, we'll take it slow at first. I'll stay with you the whole time."

Richard then paused and leaned back on the bed. "And you feel so good at night. It's wonderful exercise, and you sleep so well. And I can't wait to see Switzerland. I've never been to Europe. I took Spanish in college, but I doubt that'll do me much good. But it'll be fun to figure things out."

"Well, we'll see," she said, sitting up again.

"Hell, no!" he shouted, pushing her back on the bed.

"We've never been on a trip together, and I want us to."

"But Warwick's acting so...funny," she mumbled. "Maybe it's a trip just for the boys—you can have a good time."

"Don't worry about Warwick," Richard answered with frustration. "All he needs is the damned ski trip, you'll see. After two or three days he'll be back to normal, and you and I can do whatever we want."

They both paused, each lost in private thoughts—the perfect union having faded. Irene stood and groped for her clothing on a chair. Richard turned on the light to help her. For an instant his eyes struggled with the glare, but then adapted. And then he saw the buttocks and the long, slender legs and the silky auburn hair spilling over her taut back. He turned off the light.

"Oh, don't do that," she complained.

"I've got something to tell you," he said.

"Richard, turn the light back on—*please*," she pleaded.

"I've got something to say," he repeated, feeling a shiver himself. "And it's easier with the lights off."

"What's that?" she asked quietly.

And in the darkness he heard himself say, "I love you—I love you very much." He was afraid of what she would say, or wouldn't say. And he waited in the darkness in fear, the joy of the evening vanished. Until he heard the sound of her feet moving across the floor and met her warm, fierce embrace.

13

IT BEGAN ON Monday. Within ten minutes of the opening bell on the Cotton Exchange, futures were locked into the daily trading selling limits. That hadn't happened in almost three years.

Dazed traders wandered about the floor, gathering in small groups to find an answer. The market had retreated gradually over the previous two weeks, but never so drastically. Word was spreading of the event, and in response more and more sell orders were pouring into the floor. Was there big news? Had the government announced intervention? Was Morgan selling out?

The answers to all the questions were negative. There was no single factor that precipitated the fall. There were simply more sellers than buyers, and most of the sellers had sent small to medium-sized orders. But why so many? And why such a consensus? The floor traders always follow the orders. What did the outside world know that they didn't?

Richard usually walked to the ticker in the hallway each morning to follow the futures opening. Normally it took only two or three minutes to see the price for the day. But that morning he couldn't leave. The market had opened sharply lower, then fallen steadily until it reached

137

the daily selling limit. He was stunned; a rise to the buying limit was normal, but not this. He hurried to his office, thinking perhaps the machine was out of order, and called the floor. The telephone rang a long time, a bad omen. Finally the floor manager lifted the receiver.

"What the hell's going on?" Richard shouted above the din. "The ticker's showing limit sellers."

"It is! It is!" the manager shouted, his voice sounding unnatural. "What the hell's happening?"

"That's why I'm calling you!" Richard shouted.

"A whole lot of sellers!" the manager replied. "That's all I know. Everybody wants to sell it, and the orders are piling up. What happened? Did something big happen?"

"Not that I know of," Richard answered, anxiety sweeping his chest. "I'll call you back if I hear anything."

He hung up the telephone and paused. How long would his money hold out if this continued? The market could open limit down, with no buyers at all, for several days. After all, it had done the opposite on the way up. He grabbed the telephone and called Warwick's home. The phone rang for several irritating minutes. Finally Jason answered.

"Let me speak to War!" Richard barked. "It's important!"

"He ain't here," Jason answered slowly.

"Where is he?" Richard asked angrily.

"I axly don' know," Jason answered. "He took off early this mornin'. Didn' say nothin' to Mildred or me. Didn' want no breakfas' either."

138

"Let me speak with Irene then," Richard said impatiently.

"None of 'em's here," Jason answered. "I don' know where they be."

Richard sighed in frustration. This was information Warwick needed to know. And besides, Richard wanted to hear Warwick's opinion. He would figure it out.

A secretary knocked timidly at the door and slowly pushed it open. "Excuse me, Mr. Johnson," she said softly, "but the receptionist is flooded with calls for Mr. Morgan. Do you want to take them?"

"Who are they?" Richard asked tensely.

"Oh, it's people from all over," she answered, looking at the stack of pink slips in her hand. "The newspaper called—our office in London—Mr. Wilson from Arkansas. They're just from all over."

"Let me have them," Richard said. "Just tell them he's not in yet; he's on a trip to Texas and he'll be back this evening. Tell 'em somebody will return the call."

Richard began thumbing through the stack. It seemed the whole world was trying to reach Warwick. This had never happened before. It was like a panic. Two calls he felt should be answered immediately.

He quickly dialed the office in New York. Immediately one of the older men answered the telephone, his voice trembling.

"This is Richard!" he barked, hoping his voice sounded confident. "What do you need?"

"What am I supposed to tell all these people?" the man

asked plaintively. "The phone's ringing off the wall. They all want to know where Warwick is, and they keep asking if we're selling out. What the hell am I supposed to say?"

"Don't say anything," Richard answered as calmly as he could. "There's nothing going on that we know of. Just calm down and tell them it's business as usual, which it is."

He hung up the telephone and dialed again, this time to the biggest cotton farmer in Mississippi, with whom they had contracted to buy fourteen thousand acres of cotton production.

"Mr. Moore?" Richard asked cheerfully. "How are things going?"

"Is this Johnson?" the man asked bluntly.

"Yes, sir," Richard replied. "Warwick's down in Texas and coming back tonight. What can I do for you?"

"Where can I reach him?" he growled.

"I don't really know, Mr. Moore," Richard answered, feeling his voice quiver. "He called in this morning outside of McAllen and said he'd be in tonight."

"Well, my friends on the floor in New York say he's long up his butt in that market!" Moore shouted. "And there's talk those damn A-rabs is going to shut off our oil. He'd better have plenty of credit to buy my cotton 'cause that's going to cause the worst goddamn downturn you've ever seen—it'll shut this country *down*."

"It's all hedged, Mr. Moore," Richard answered, his head feeling light. "Every pound of it."

"They say the damn fool's bought everything in sight!" Moore argued. "That looked smart last week, but it looks like *shit* right now. I've contracted for my seed, equipment, fertilizer, and everything else; he's got to be ready to buy my goddamn cotton!"

"We are, Mr. Moore," Richard replied. "Why, I'm meeting with the banks at lunch. They have all the information, and our line of credit is completely sound. There's no problem, Mr. Moore. We can weather whatever storm comes our way."

Moore hung up without saying a word. Richard stared at the receiver, overwhelmed by Moore's ferocity. He was a powerful man in the world of farming, and he would be known and listened to by all the rest. Where in the hell was Warwick?

The private dining room atop the bank was hushed and serene—the first island of calm Richard had encountered all morning. The bankers—the chairmen of two banks, the president of another, and various subordinates—talked amiably among themselves. Richard was glad to have a moment to himself, so many things were happening so swiftly. He knew he had to perform perfectly before these people, men who wouldn't have known his name just months before.

He was relieved that no one had mentioned the events that morning at the Exchange. Almost all of Warwick's liquidity was tied up in the merchant operation and outside investments. Everyone knew he was active on the

Exchange, but that was supposedly to hedge the merchant activities. They surely didn't know about the mammoth speculative position he had acquired; Warwick had hidden it too well. If they knew, they would certainly become uneasy, even to the point of panic. It was important to keep them contented for several days, to give Warwick time to weather the short adjustment in price that now looked quite possible.

The chairman of the lead bank finished his story about a famous hunting dog and cleared his throat. The room became silent—Richard knew bankers liked long lunches and short meetings.

"Richard, thank you for meeting with us today," he began in the practiced, relaxed southern accent used by the Memphis establishment. "We felt that all of us needed to get together in the same room to review what Morgan & Son is doing. Frankly," he chuckled, "it sounds like you boys bought all the cotton in the world!" The others laughed politely, until the chairman again cleared his throat. "We're not at all worried about your ability to sell the cotton—in fact, you've supplied us with the contracts to the mills and overseas importers—and we're also not too worried about your ability to carry a good portion of inventory if you have to. We're happy with your financial condition and—speaking for our bank at least—feel the line of credit is deserved and reasonable. But... because it's substantially larger than you ever asked for before, we feel it prudent to be...reassured...about any other activities the company's involved in. Now, for instance, the warehouses you bought here in town look sound, as. does the farmland down in Louisiana. You boys know that business, and we're comfortable with it. But there're some others—I forget—but I believe there's a fairly big oil and gas deal and substantial real estate investments, things we really don't know much about and, frankly, don't make much music to a banker in Memphis." The others agreed with a variety of short sounds. "We just want to be sure you keep your liquidity high, or high enough, in case you need to carry more cotton than you're able to sell. I'm not saying we want to put any *harness* on you, but I do think—and I'm sure I speak for all of us—that we'd like to see you slow down on these outside investments for a while, at least until we see that your selling program's going as planned."

The other bankers signaled with smiles both to the chairman and to Richard their endorsement of the older man's presentation. For a fleeting, perverse moment, Richard wished he could tell them the awesome truth of the futures position.

"Let me ask just a couple of...things," one of the subordinates interjected haltingly. Richard recognized the tall, steely-eyed man, and he held his breath. "How... how are you...calculating your hedges against the production? I mean, if this weather keeps up, you might have sold too much in New York—yet you've got to be sure you sold enough futures to protect yourselves against a price drop, as unlikely as that might seem."

Richard's stomach tightened. If the truth were to be

143

out, it would be now. "I wish Warwick could have been here today—he sends his regrets, by the way—," Richard began. "He's the one who could best explain the hedging formula. I can tell you that we're confident it works—it always has—*and* that it's in place. We are expecting a bull market next year, so the hedge position might look a little light. But we can always adjust if there's a break." Richard held his breath. The words were all so new to him, he hoped they came out convincingly.

The inquisitor cleared his throat and twice aborted his next question. Finally he asked, "You generated an ... impressive amount of cash over the past several months— at least we've seen an increase at our shop. We haven't gotten your year-end statement yet, but is there something ... unusual ... which is generating so much cash?"

"Well," Richard answered with a big grin. "I guess you guys are just getting more than your share! I wish you wouldn't bring it up around these other fellows!"

The rest of the table laughed with disinterest, and Richard quickly turned toward the chairman. "I'll pass all of this along to Warwick," he said, looking the older man in the eye, "and I can assure you that we're going to ... take a *vacation* for a while from the outside investments." He paused while the others nodded in agreement. "I could use one anyway."

Richard jogged the few blocks to his office. It was cold and damp, with even lower temperatures, perhaps snow, predicted. But he still felt relieved, and proud. He was sure the bankers were satisfied, and he and Warwick had gained enough breathing room. He turned the corner onto Front Street and noticed a small cluster of men standing in front of the building. He nodded as he walked past, recognizing a few old faces in the business. No one responded as he opened the door and ascended the rickety stairs.

As soon as he walked through the top door, the receptionist whipped off her earphones and pleaded, "Mr. Johnson! What am I supposed to do with all these calls? Some of them are *cursing* me!"

"Just . . . just tell them everyone's occupied. All the calls will be returned later," he answered, unnerved by the girl's hysteria. "Everything's going to be all right."

He walked down the hall to his office and slipped inside. He took off his coat and then caught sight of the ski sweater he had bought. "I guess I won't be needing that," he mumbled, anger rising up that Warwick had left the day before their trip. But it made no difference, he told himself; they couldn't leave anyway until the markets calmed down.

He sat down and called the trading floor. Market hours were over, but he wanted to hear if there were any new developments. "Nothing," the manager told him. "But rumors are rife that Warwick's selling."

"Tell 'em they're nuts!" Richard replied. "It's impossible without my knowing it."

He hung up the receiver and dialed again. After several rings, Jason answered. They were still not home, and no one had called. Richard slammed down the receiver. He then called Irwin and asked to meet him at a bar on the way home. Irwin was glad to leave as well. He too was having a bad day.

Richard stood and grabbed his coat and the sweater. There was nothing more he could do at the office with Warwick out of reach. What was he supposed to tell all the callers? He knew nothing. He told the receptionist he would be at home in case Mr. Morgan or Miss Moody called, and bounded down the stairs. He opened the lower door and was immediately confronted by an even larger gathering of Front Street cotton men.

"Where's Warwick?" one of them shouted with a touch of irony. "Gone deer huntin'?"

"He's down in Texas," Richard answered, threading along the edge of the crowd. "He said this morning he was on his way back."

"Who's selling all the cotton?" another asked coyly, certainly knowing he wouldn't get an answer.

"A little profit-taking, I guess," Richard said with a smile. "It can't go up every day."

No one else spoke, but they all turned to watch as he headed toward the garage. He could feel the animosity, and a wave of shame overcame him. He was lying to them—men who were the backbone of the cotton community—and he felt himself a usurper, a carpetbagger. But what could he do? He didn't know what the market was doing. That was Warwick's job. So what else could he say?

The drive out Union Avenue was pleasant. There was no traffic, and he was going to escape for a few hours with his friend—maybe even meet a girl to talk with. There was nothing wrong with that; he had always been honest with Irene. He found a parking place directly in front of the bar at Overton Square and sprinted inside. It was early and the crowd was thin. He spied Irwin at the bar with an arm around a waitress.

"Hey, Rich!" Irwin shouted. "Come over and meet my new fiancée!"

"To hell with *that*," the girl answered. "I don't even know your name."

"We have to have some excuse to go to bed," Irwin cooed. "I don't sleep with just anybody."

"Go 'way, creep," she replied, breaking away.

"Ah, you win some, you lose some," Irwin sighed. "How's your love life?"

"Pretty good," Richard smiled, taking a stool. "I'll buy you a drink."

"I could use one," Irwin answered in a lower voice. "Thing's ain't going too good."

"What's the matter?" Richard asked, signaling the bartender.

"Oh, they say this oil thing's going to drive up inflation and cause a recession," he answered glumly. "That should mean tighter money, and none of our lenders wants to talk to us. Things have been going really well too. I guess it couldn't last forever."

"Cotton was limit sellers today," Richard blurted,

relieved he could talk about his fears with somebody he trusted.

"Damn, what happened?" Irwin asked, leaning forward.

"Nobody really knows," Richard answered. "Maybe it's what the guy said in the paper. I don't understand it. There's going to be a big short crop."

"Yeah, but if you ain't got the money, old boy, you can't play the jukebox," Irwin answered, lifting his beer.

"I got a pretty big position too," Richard said quietly.

"Well, get the hell out!" Irwin urged him. "At least until you find out what's happening."

"Well, I couldn't today," Richard explained. "It was limit sellers; nothing was trading. Besides, Warwick's been managing the account."

"What does he say?" Irwin asked.

"Oh, hell, he's pulled one of his disappearing acts," Richard moaned. "I haven't spoken to him all day."

"Where'd he go?" Irwin asked.

"I don't *know*," Richard answered. "He does that every once in a while. Just disappears. I don't know where he goes—Las Vegas? Fishing in the Keys? Some motel with a babe? I don't know."

"That's not exactly Harvard Business School management technique," Irwin mumbled in his glass. "I told you he was nuts."

"Yeah, and we were supposed to go skiing tomorrow," Richard continued. "I was really looking forward to that."

148

"Where to?" Irwin asked, eyeing a new girl who entered the door.

"Switzerland," Richard answered. "I've never been there."

"Well, get yourself out of the cotton market—with your profits—and take yourself to Switzerland," Irwin said, signaling for a new beer. "And now that we've gotten all the ordinary problems out of the way, let's move on to the big one. Let's get drunk!"

"Suits me!" Richard laughed. "It's been a long time."

The music was loud, and the flashing, blinking lights, irritating. Richard hadn't eaten, and his head was beginning to throb. Irwin was talking with two girls, one of whom stole furtive glances his way. She was dressed like a teenager, but was certainly older than he. She had long, very blonde hair and wore a tight T-shirt with "I Do It" emblazoned on the front. She smiled, and he knew her teeth were too perfect to be her own. He remembered those country girls back home whom one met at the community dances and roadhouses. They were divorced or deserted, or simply had never found a man. They were the saddest people he had ever known, sadder even than the old and sick or the very poor or the neglected young. For those knew their condition and could work against it, but the honky-tonk ladies never seemed to know what they were looking for or where to find it. So they went to the bars in search of men like himself, and used themselves expensively for a few hours of tinsel and twenty minutes of lies.

The bartender delivered another drink, and Richard attempted to protest. The girl took the opportunity to lean his way and smile again broadly. "Don't any of the men around here like to dance?" she asked, tripping suddenly on the leg of Irwin's stool.

"You're doing a pretty good job yourself," Richard answered, touching her elbow in support.

"Shit!" she muttered, looking to see if she had spilled her drink. "These *goddamn* shoes is too tight!"

She composed herself and then looked up at Richard's face. He said nothing, so the two continued to stare at one another in intimacy. Richard knew he was supposed to say something that would allow her to become more forward, but his head hurt too much to make the effort.

"You're a whole lot of fun," she said, moving toward the stool next to him.

"That's what all the girls say," Richard answered, wondering suddenly where Irene might be.

"You're not against having a good time, are you?" she asked, arranging herself on the seat.

"Naw, and never was," Richard answered in a country accent.

"Then let's dance," she asked, lifting her face close to his.

Richard was suddenly bewildered, a wave of concern for Irene sweeping over him. But there was also something else—the room seemed to be spinning and his stomach was beginning to hurt.

"I bet you're a real good dancer," the girl continued. "I bet you can really cut a rug."

"I...I...don't know," Richard answered faintly.

"Well, why don't we try," she asked, placing a hand on his buttocks. "I bet you can dance slow real good."

"I...I'm going to be sick," he answered.

14

RICHARD'S HEAD THROBBED, even while lying half asleep in the darkened bedroom. He knew it would become worse if he got up, but he also knew he couldn't take the day off. A crisis was in the making, and he had to go to work. So he dragged himself to a sitting position and held his head between his hands. He felt ashamed and depressed, and anxiety was building rapidly.

He stood and stumbled to the bathroom. He placed two Alka-Seltzers in a glass and watched them foam. After he drank them, he looked out the window. It was snowing. He took a robe and made his way down the narrow staircase. The living room was dark, so he whipped open the curtains. He muttered an oath upon seeing how deeply the snow had already drifted along the walkway and drive.

He lifted the telephone receiver and called the office. The news was as bad as he had expected—the futures were down the limit for a second straight day. The government had announced the probability of a severe energy shortage for months—perhaps years—to come, and all markets, everywhere, were plunging. He replaced the receiver and again put his face in his hands. He was going to have trouble getting out of his positions, and how long would his money hold out? Oh, where was Warwick? He would surely know what to do. He always did.

He picked up the telephone and called the number at Warwick's estate. Jason answered and said Warwick wasn't back, but that Sammie and Irene had returned. He asked to speak with Irene.

"Hello!" she chirped. "I was hoping you would call."

"Careful, careful," Richard moaned in earnest. "I've got the worst hangover in the history of the world."

"Serves you right," she answered. "You didn't call me last night."

"I called you *ten times* yesterday," he growled, "but nobody was home."

"I was out shopping," she answered, munching on something. "Didn't get back till around six."

"I went out with Irwin," Richard explained. "We didn't get in until three this morning, and I feel awful."

"I can come over and bring you something to eat," she offered.

"No, no, I've got to get to the office," he answered. "Listen, where the hell is Warwick? There's an emergency going on, and I need him bad."

"I don't know where he is," she answered. "Let me ask Sammie."

A few seconds later Sammie lifted an extension and, in his deep, rough voice, shouted, "A little too much party, eh?"

"A lot too much," Richard answered, unable to fake a laugh. "Say, where's War? There's some real shit going on in this cotton market."

"You're telling me," Sammie answered. "I got a

margin call from my broker this morning. How long's this thing going to last?"

"War knows all the answers," Richard answered. "And we've gotta get hold of him. You have any ideas?"

"Sure don't," Sammie answered. "I haven't seen him in a couple of days. I suppose he's with some babe somewhere. But don't worry. He's like an old dog—he always finds his way home."

"Well, it's damn important," Richard said. "Tell him to call me the minute you hear from him."

"I will," he replied. "Here's Irene."

"You want to do something tonight?" he asked.

"With all this snow on the way, I'm afraid to leave the house," she answered. "Besides I need to do my hair. You want to come out here?"

"Well, let me see how it goes," he answered. "I don't think I'm going to be feeling any better. Maybe I should just stay home and sleep it off."

"Call me anyway," she cooed. "I miss you."

"Me too, lover," he answered. "I'll call."

The drive to the office was tedious. The rush hour was long over, but most motorists, unused to driving in the snow, nervously inched along. Richard turned on the radio, and all the stations were reporting the impending oil embargo. The stock market was off over twenty points in the first hour, and the president was asking Congress for emergency powers. To make things even worse, they were forecasting heavy snow all night. Warwick was right about one thing—the weather in the South was changing. But what good would that do now? There were other factors seizing the national attention.

The scene at the office was frantic. The reception room was packed with people—farmers, merchants, newsmen, the curious. The receptionist was obviously relieved to see Richard. The office manager threw up his hands in a prayerful gesture. Richard smiled at everyone and began making his way through the mass toward his office.

One newsman stepped in his path and smiled. "We understand Warwick Morgan has disappeared, Mr. Johnson. Do you suspect foul play?"

The words struck Richard like a brick. Foul play? How oddly out of context it sounded. Warwick was simply on one of his frequent sojourns. Foul play? What could that mean?

"You've been watching too many movies," Richard answered with a smile. "Mr. Morgan's doing fine."

"Then where is he?" an older man in work clothes asked. "He bought all mah cotton. Am I goin' to git mah money?"

"Everything's in order," Richard answered, reaching the hallway. "Everybody's going to be paid."

"We heard he's committed suicide," another newsman shouted, just before a camera flashed.

Richard blinked and shook his head with a grin. "I just finished talking with him, and I think he'd be amused to hear about his poor health."

"Then you know where he is?" another one shouted.

"Of course, of course," Richard answered, without looking back. He was exhausted when he shut the door to his office.

The telephone rang instantly. It was the office manager. "Empire Trading's been calling you all morning," he said. "I think you'd better give them a ring."

A shiver raced through Richard's chest. With the market falling, he was surely running out of money. And he only had a few thousand in his savings account. How could he cover the losses if prices continued their plunge? Oh, where was Warwick? And why did the bastard have to leave now?

He grabbed the receiver again and called the trading floor. "Phillip?" he asked. "This is Richard. How does it look up there now?"

"Pretty grim, Rich," the floor manager answered. "We're still down the limit, and sell orders are pouring in by the hundreds. They estimate the pool at five thousand contracts, and they're still coming in. At this rate we could be limit-locked for two or three days. I don't know anybody who's short."

"Damn," Richard moaned, his head throbbing again. "Call me if anything comes up. By the way, there're a lot of rumors around about War. I just finished talking with him, and he thinks this is a technical correction. We're in good shape to weather the storm, so don't worry. It's really amusing. Why, one guy even asked if he'd committed suicide. I told him War's too chicken shit!"

They both laughed and said goodbye. Richard replaced

the receiver, the smile vanishing immediately. Would Warwick possibly commit suicide? Hell, no. He's just on one of his crazy trips. But why hasn't he called? Surely he's read a newspaper. He knows the natives are coming over the walls. If there had been an accident, the police would certainly have called. Maybe he's relishing the whole event, letting the lower types in life get worried and sweaty. He's probably holed up somewhere laughing his head off over all the panic and furor. And he plans to come back in glory—and scare the hell out of all the weak in spirit. But, by God, he'd better hurry. The firm can stand a few more days of this, but can't take it forever. He had lied to the banks; not everything was hedged. Someday the margins would have to be met at the Exchange. But, even worse, at some point hundreds of farmers would have to be paid for their cotton. But that wouldn't happen until fall, and there was plenty of time for War to work his magic. He was just setting a trap.

Richard knew he had to call the manager at Empire Trading. To avoid him could further fuel the rumors that the firm was in trouble. Yet Richard hesitated. It was easier not to know the truth, easier to ignore the problem. He finally reached for the telephone and dialed.

A clerk answered, and Richard asked for Mr. Mc-Donald. "Hello?" the man asked breathlessly. "Is that Johnson?"

"Yes, it is," Richard answered confidently. "What can I do for you?"

"This account of yours is having a little trouble," the

older man blurted. "We probably need some more margin."

Richard felt rage build up quickly, but suppressed it. He had to keep his head. "It's still positive, isn't it?" he asked. "There's still a credit balance, right?"

"Yeah, yeah," the manager answered, as if in a daze. "But we'd like some more. We don't think this thing's over; it could go a lot lower."

"Wait a minute, wait a minute," Richard replied calmly. "This is *my* account and *my* money. I'm the guy trading, right?"

"Yeah, yeah, young fellow, but it's my job to keep the accounts liquid," he answered.

"Now, wait a minute! When the account gets into debit, I'll send the money," Richard said. "Besides, you have Morgan's guarantee on the damned thing."

"Well, I don't know how good that's gonna be—from all the rumors," the old man answered. "And don't forget, this is *your* account. We've got to look to you for the money."

"How much is in the account?" Richard asked, ashamed he had reminded the man of Warwick's guarantee.

"About four thousand dollars," the old man answered after a pause.

Richard was stunned. He had lost a fortune. He couldn't believe it. "That's impossible!" he gasped.

"You put on another twenty contracts just two days ago," the manager replied. "It's right here—"

158

"Call me tomorrow if you need the money," Richard ordered. "I'm busy as hell right now. Call me tomorrow if you need the money!"

Richard was in trouble, and he knew it. His whole body seemed to weaken, as if he had received a blow to the stomach. The market would surely trade lower the next morning. But maybe—*maybe*—it would bottom out and rally later in the session. He knew he had to prepare himself to meet the margin call. But how? He didn't have the money to cover another limit move. He moaned and placed his head on the desk.

If only Warwick would appear, he told himself. Surely he would be able to help him with the margin money. But, more important, he would know what the hell was going on. He was sick of this business, with all its tensions and anxiety. There was nothing else he could do—it was now all a question of the price of cotton the next morning. Richard lifted his head and decided to leave. He'd go home and fix a drink and sit in a hot tub. Given time, everything would work out.

The crowd had deserted the reception room, leaving behind empty coffee cups and bits and scraps of paper. As his hand reached for the door, the office manager appeared.

"You off?" he asked, barely masking his concern.

"Yeah," Richard answered nonchalantly. "I 'over-indulged' at a party last night and need a little nap."

"Well, you'll be in tomorrow?" the man asked timidly.

"Why, of course," Richard answered, suddenly realizing how shaken the man was. "I'll be in bright and early. But if you have trouble with the snow, don't worry. Just get here when you can. The streets from my house should be clear."

"Fine," the man replied, his whole body relaxing. "It's just that ... it's just so ... unsettling around here, when no one's in."

Richard shuddered and pushed through the door.

The ride home was treacherous. The snow fell faster and faster, then turned into slush and ice under the crunch of the early rush. At one intersection there was a collision and at another a traffic jam. Ice began accumulating on Richard's wipers, and twice he had to stop to clean them. By the time he reached his own street, he was bursting with frustration—trapped at every turn, it seemed, by giant forces grossly indifferent to his condition.

He pulled in the driveway and slipped and slid toward the house. It was the worst snow he had seen since childhood, and if it continued, there would be difficulty leaving later. He parked the car where he could move it easily and hopped through the snow to the porch. When he opened the door, he saw Irwin and a petite young blonde girl lighting a fire.

"Hey, big fella!" Irwin shouted over his shoulder. "Meet Cheryl. She's my solution to the snowstorm."

"How ya doin'?" Richard mumbled, suddenly envious of the pretty girl and, more so, of Irwin's lack of care. He wasn't in trouble, and probably never would be. Maybe that's the way to organize one's life—just keep the party going.

"Cheryl lives around the corner," Irwin announced, straightening up. "That's a real piece of luck, isn't it? We're going to wander over there and have a little dinner in a few minutes. Wanna come with us?"

"Oh, that sounds great," Richard answered. "But after last night I think I'm going to fix some eggs and hit the hay early. Thanks, though."

"At least come down and have a drink with us," Irwin chirped, watching Richard climb the stairs. "We've gotta celebrate—this is supposed to be the biggest snowfall in Memphis' history."

"I will," Richard answered. "Let me take a bath first."

In his room, he wearily shed his jacket and tie. They were the trappings of success—cashmere and silk. And he suddenly saw them as frauds—one was supposed to be rich to have them. He then removed the rest of his clothes and trudged to the bathroom. It was cold, and the hot water steamed as it gushed from the faucet. He sat down on the toilet and placed his head in his hands. Things always get better, his father used to say. No matter how bleak things might seem today, you'll laugh and enjoy life again. And Richard knew that was right. Sometime in the next few days everything would correct itself. Warwick would return, and the markets would slow down, and he'd work out his problem at Empire. He just had to be courageous, and everything would work out.

Slowly he lowered his body into the stinging water, but

161

it wasn't until his neck submerged that he realized how tense he had become. The water was the next best thing to jogging; he could feel the muscles release and his breathing become deeper and more regular. That was all he needed—a little time to himself, a short respite from the pressures upon him. He took a bar of soap and began bathing. He remembered his body and its condition, its health and attraction to others. There was more to life than simply becoming a big shot. There were other values. Everything would turn out all right. He would laugh again.

Richard wore a long robe when he returned to the living room. Surely Cheryl had seen men wearing a robe before—probably seen them wearing a lot less. He lay down on the couch facing the fire, bathing in its warmth and simplicity. Cheryl brought him a drink and placed it on the coffee table. He took a long sip, which evoked the bitter tastes of the night before. But, he reasoned, a little "hair of the dog" would probably help.

He closed his eyes and listened to Irwin and the girl chatter inanely in front of the fireplace. Irwin had a wonderful way with women, probably because he truly enjoyed their company. He would talk about anything they wished, and always with genuine interest. And they in return felt comfortable—accepted and whole. No wonder they all wanted to sleep with him; it was a logical confirmation that their lives had purpose and value.

"I read the commodity page this evening," Irwin said, his voice betraying sympathy. "I know you probably feel like shit, but I want you to know you're not...all alone. I've been a loser before too, and, boy, does it hurt! You probably don't want to talk about it—"

"No, I don't," Richard answered with a laugh. "But I appreciate it. Everything's going to work out all right. It's just a little setback."

"Well, if there's anything I can do, besides lend you money," Irwin joked, "I'll be glad to help."

"Thanks, Ir," Richard answered, settling deeper into the couch. "Right now, I could use a little nap."

Irwin and Cheryl left quietly, leaving a bottle of whiskey and a bucket of ice on the coffee table. Richard quickly slipped into a deep and tingling daze, as if his mind were being drugged, pulled away from its connection with nature. And as he moved farther and farther from the light and sound, he recalled the things he should have done. Vaguely he remembered he wanted to call his mother; that would give him strength and encouragement. And he should have called Irene; he wished she were there. And he should sit down with pad and pencil and calculate exactly what was happening, not only with the business, but also with his personal life. But he couldn't—he was falling faster and faster—until everything was gone.

15

DURING THE LONG, cold night the world became transformed. Huge masses of northern air invaded the Mississippi Valley, bringing with them gruesome, never before experienced, temperatures. Snow and slush swirled and dashed, up and down, coating all things exposed with thick, vulnerable moisture. And then as quickly as the storm began, it rushed farther south, leaving every vestige of nature in a near vacuum of cold and thick crystalline ice.

Richard awoke grudgingly from his sleep on the sofa. The fire was long dead and the room bitterly cold. He curled up under his robe, trying to protect his feet from the temperature's nip, but finally surrendered and sat up. He felt completely rested after the long sleep. He knew it was early because light was barely creeping through the draperies. It was good to get up early, he told himself. It would be important to be fresh and alert.

He rose slowly, pulling his robe around him. It would be pleasant to rebuild the fire, he thought, but dangerous to leave it unattended. Instead, he walked to the thermostat in the hallway and moved it higher. He squinted to see the temperature, but it was too dark. He then turned toward the kitchen. He had enough time to make coffee in the percolator, and that always tasted better.

He flicked on the light and nothing happened. The bulb must be out, he thought, as he walked toward one of the cabinets. He found the coffee and slowly ran water from the faucet into the pot. When it was full, he inserted the parts and filled it with grounds. The electric plug was bent, so he straightened it with his fingers before sliding it into the socket. That's when he yawned and looked out the window into the nascent dawn.

Richard gasped at what he saw. The whole of nature was entombed in a covering of thick, hard, clear ice. Limbs on trees and bushes were contorted awkwardly under the weight, giving the impression at first of torture. Even the ground had not escaped. A thick skin of ice covered the deep, new-fallen snow. And no creature moved—no bird nor dog nor man.

How in God's name was he going to get to the office? And he had to get there. He rushed back into the living room, trying light after light. All were out. The power was gone. Quickly, he lifted the telephone. That too was dead. That meant the heat was off—no wonder it was so cold. He quickly began building a fire.

As the flames began to flicker, Richard hugged himself for warmth, trying to decide what he would do, how he would establish communications. He ran up the stairs to the bedroom to find his radio with batteries. He brought it back down the stairs and turned it on. All of the stations carried news of the storm. The entire region was under siege—roads were closed, power was out, telephones were down—and there was more snow on the way. The National Guard had been mobilized.

Richard cursed and wandered back into the kitchen. He unplugged the helpless coffeepot and lifted some milk from the refrigerator. He drank from the carton, desperately thinking of what to do next. Finally, he decided there was only one thing to do—he would walk to one of the main streets and try to hitch a ride to town. Surely the telephones to the business community would be restored. If nothing else, he could get to a telephone at a gas station. The Exchange would be opening in an hour. At least he could place an order to sell his contracts, just in the event of a miracle.

He ran up the stairs and took a shower—the gas water heater was working. He shaved and put on his warmest clothes; the radio said the temperature was below zero. He returned to the kitchen and made himself a peanut butter and jelly sandwich. His stomach was already tight, but he knew he would need some nourishment to brave the weather. He then put on his warmest coat, but not before placing a screen in front of the fireplace. The way his luck was running, the house would burn down. He then stepped out onto the front porch, and felt the sharp, ugly bite of the bitterly cold air.

The world was ominously quiet as he made his way down the driveway; nothing moved beneath its shroud of ice. The going was rough, his feet cracking through the ice covering and plunging into the deep snow. Once he considered turning back, but he had no choice. He had to make it to the office.

He finally reached the deserted street, which was glazed with almost sheer ice. He tried walking on it, but immediately fell hard on his back. For a second he saw stars, then had difficulty breathing. He lay there gasping, the tears in his eyes rapidly freezing. Finally he was able to roll over. Somehow he had lost a glove, and the ice cruelly tore at his hand. He struggled to his feet and again fell, twisting a leg. So he sat there, wondering what in the world he was going to do next. And then he heard himself sob—and he knew he was crying. He was losing everything he had in life, and he was helpless against the forces allied against him. He wished he could simply run away, escape all his problems, but he didn't know how. He was at their mercy.

Then something intruded on Richard's resignation. There was a sound, a churning, in the distance. He ungloved his other hand and began massaging his blurred eyes. Only then through the stinging film could he make out an object, a vehicle, slipping and swerving down the roadbed of ice toward him. At first he sat totally captured by the image of the machine careening forward. At least there was life. At least someone else was surviving against the forces. He watched as it grew nearer and nearer, its angry roar growing louder and louder. Finally he realized he would have to move if the machine continued its course, so he dragged himself painfully toward the curb. Perhaps the driver would stop and give him assistance.

167

The machine looked familiar, but he couldn't remember where he had seen it before. It was a brown Landrover, which suddenly began spinning in an effort to stop. Its wheels churned, spitting up showers of ice, until, as suddenly as it had appeared, it came to a halt. With a jolt, the side door flew open. There was Warwick.

Richard's heart leaped, and he began struggling once again to gain his feet.

"Just crawl on over, asshole!" Warwick shouted above the growl of the engine. "Here, take my hand."

"Where the hell you been?" Richard shouted, as he pulled himself on all fours toward the door. "I thought you'd *never* come back."

"It's lucky I saw you," Warwick answered. "Damn, you can't stop this crazy thing!"

Richard's eyes again clouded over, but he felt the hand grasp his own, and he knew he was safe. Warwick was back, and everything would return to normal. His foot slipped as he raised up, and his knee smashed against the pavement. The pain was dulled by the cold, but Richard knew it would hurt later. Finally he lifted himself into the moist, cozy cabin. It was as if he had returned from a long trip.

"What the hell were you doing out here?" Warwick yelled. "It's well below zero; a man could freeze in twenty minutes!"

"I had to get to the office," Richard explained, rubbing his eyes. "There was no other way."

Warwick jammed the gear forward, and the powerful

machine lurched into action. He drove it as with a vengeance, whipping the wheel from side to side. At Richard's driveway, he shoved the gear into the four-wheel drive and lunged toward the house. Richard spread his hand on the seat to keep his balance, and then felt the clammy barrel of a .38.

"What the hell's that for?" he muttered in disbelief.

"Never mind," Warwick answered, sliding the machine to a halt. "Just get in there and pack for the trip."

"The trip?" Richard asked, his eyes passing between Warwick and the pistol. "What trip?"

"Switzerland!" Warwick answered impatiently. "We're goin' skiin', remember?"

"For God's sake, we can't go skiing," Richard replied. "The market's...puking its *guts!* We need to be here. We can't leave now!"

"Everything's taken care of," Warwick answered, his head falling to his hands on the steering wheel. "Just get your butt in there and pack. Please, we're late."

"We can't get out anyway, War," Richard argued. "Everything's closed. The airport is surely closed."

"Not to private aircraft," Warwick answered, wearily. "Get packed."

Richard noticed Warwick's appearance. He hadn't shaved in several days, and dark circles cradled his eyes. It seemed he had lost weight.

"Where have you been, by the way?" Richard asked, resentment welling up. "It's been rough around here—"

"Look, we don't have time," Warwick answered impatiently. "Get your damned *clothes.*"

"But...but...what about the firm?" Richard asked.

"The company's all right," Warwick mumbled, biting his lower lip.

"It can't be," Richard argued. "We've got—"

"The company's gone," Warwick replied quietly, his head turned toward the window.

In the silence, both could feel the pulse of the Landrover. Warwick continued his glazed stare, while Richard tried to remember whether he heard the right words.

"Gone?" Richard whispered. "What does that mean?"

"Look!" Warwick replied, opening his door and stepping outside. "We've *got* to get going! Let's get your stuff. We're in a hurry!"

Richard opened his door and slid around the Landrover. "The company can't be gone," he said, slipping for a second. "The market's only been down for two days; that's not enough to take us under."

Warwick said nothing, but instead stomped onto the porch and reached for the front door.

"What do you mean 'gone'?" Richard asked. "What's happened I don't know about?"

Warwick proceeded through the door, not bothering to shake the snow from his shoes. "Where's your suitcase?" he shouted. "You live like a field hand."

Richard was totally confused. What the hell was Warwick talking about—the company gone? Why were they going skiing in the face of such a crisis? He wanted answers and was becoming angry because they weren't forthcoming. "I'm not going anywhere," he said, knocking the snow from his boots, "until I find out what the hell's happening."

Warwick proceeded up the stairs. "Which room is yours?" he asked. "Right or left?"

"Warwick. Goddammit! You've got to answer me!" Richard insisted, following him. "Or I'm not going anywhere."

In the bedroom, Warwick tried the lights. "Don't you ever buy light bulbs?" he asked.

"The power's out," Richard answered, opening the blinds.

"Now, where's the suitcase?" Warwick roared.

Exasperated, Richard felt the urge to laugh. His old buddy was just being his crazy old self. Everything was all right. Warwick was just in one of his moods. "Why are we going to Switzerland?" he asked, sitting on the side of the bed. "It might be a little more *convenient* to go to Colorado."

"To get the money," Warwick answered quietly, opening the closet door.

"The money?" Richard asked. "What money?"

Warwick pulled a large suitcase from the closet and threw it on the bed next to Richard. "Better bring a jockstrap, Tiger," he mumbled. "It might get a little... athletic."

Richard sat and watched Warwick move first from the

closet and then to the bureau. "Nice sweater—want it?" he asked. "Better bring these blue jeans—European ladies like 'em. You can pack your own underwear." And the longer Warwick wandered around the bedroom mumbling and tossing clothes into the suitcase, the more Richard began to realize that something really had changed. Warwick wasn't his old self. He was serious about going to Switzerland. He...he wasn't going to stand and fight.

"What's happened?" Richard finally asked. "Why are we running away?"

Warwick paused and stared at a necktie he had just lifted from Richard's drawer. He then began running the fingers of his free hand across his nose, caressing the skin tenderly, as might a man with a woman's breast. He then dropped his hands to his side and turned toward Richard.

"We were right, you know," he began slowly, his voice normal and confident. "They ain't gonna plant any cotton this spring. The crop's gonna be real short." Again he paused and examined the necktie. "But something else has happened, something I never dreamed of. Nobody did. And that's the problem. Those goddamn Arabs are going to get together and squeeze the hell out of us. Oil's goin' to go sky-high—fifty dollars a barrel, maybe a thousand. And oil's...more important...than cotton."

"Well, we've got a couple of oil wells," Richard argued, hoping to encourage his friend.

"Oh, you idiot," Warwick mumbled to himself. "You should have stayed a lawyer. How in the hell will one or two small wells help with cotton at forty cents a pound or less?"

Richard felt faint, and his mind went blank. Warwick had said it with such resignation. He was always right, and that meant forty-cent cotton. There was no way to survive. He was gone. He couldn't think of anything to say. He could do nothing but fight the nausea in his stomach.

"I bought some Swiss franc futures at the IMM awhile back," Warwick monotoned. "Several million, just in case. Took delivery last Thursday. All paid for. Zurich delivery. That's why we have to go skiin'."

Richard sat with his mouth agape. It couldn't be happening. He wasn't really hearing what he was hearing. Finally he leaned over and shook his head vigorously. "This...this..."

"It's in your name," Warwick continued.

Richard's head slowly rose, his eyes widening. He began turning his head from side to side.

"I had to do it," Warwick said quietly. "They'd trace my name in a second. It'll take 'em a couple of months to figure you out. By that time we'll have the dough and be long gone. It's our only shot."

"That's...criminal," Richard whispered, his head still moving.

"Listen, Rich," Warwick hissed. "It's already too late. We're both in the shitter, and that means you won't ever practice law again. They don't like bankrupts wanderin' around law courts these days. Besides, we've already done it, so how can it get worse? Let's cut and run, man."

"Crime?" Richard whispered.

"We did it together," Warwick announced. "That's what they'll think."

The silence roared in Richard's ears. He knew everything was now different. He was in fundamental trouble, and he didn't know what to do. He could call Arnold—that was all he could do. He was in big trouble, criminal trouble, and he was helpless.

"I won't go," he heard himself say. "Leave the house."

"She's coming," Warwick said softly.

Again the silence thundered in his ears. There was too much to think about, too many things happening. His head stung with anxiety.

"She'll do anything I say," Warwick continued quietly. "She can't resist what's between my legs."

With that Richard leaped from the bed and swung wildly at Warwick's head. Warwick ducked and stepped to the other side of the room.

"She loves it," he continued. "She used to talk to it. We even had a name for it. And that was my *baby* she aborted."

Again Richard lunged, rage overwhelming him. Why was he so inept? Why couldn't he strike the beast?

"But that was before you came along," Warwick sallied, sidestepping another blind swing. "She'll do whatever I—and Sammie—tell her to do."

Richard turned hysterically, looking for some object, some weapon, to help.

"She's yours," Warwick whispered. "She always will be—if you come to Switzerland. That's all you have to do.

Just come skiin'. That's real natural. We've been talking about a vacation."

And Richard stopped whirling. She was all he had left. Everything else was gone. Everything.

"Now, pack the underwear, asshole," Warwick said. "We don't have much time."

16

THE AIRCRAFT WAGED its struggle through the blackened night, its giant body bumping and swaying in conflict with the elements. To Richard the machine seemed almost human, twisting and groaning in its powerful effort to overcome a hostile nature.

He couldn't sleep, despite the exhausting events of the day. Instead, he simply tossed in his seat, his mind obsessed with fear and self-loathing. He had almost changed his mind before leaving—he had forgotten his passport, and they were forced to return to the house. He had stood in the darkened bedroom for endless minutes, alone finally, weighing the alternatives. But when Warwick blew his horn, he knew it was his only hope for a normal life. To stay behind meant bankruptcy—and almost certain disbarment. And if Warwick were good on his threat, he could even go to jail. There was nothing illegal about leaving the country; they had planned to go skiing, after all. But what was his role in the currency futures transaction? What would happen with the money? All he knew was that he could decide later what was right and wrong.

He turned and looked at Irene, curled asleep in the big seat next to him. He finally knew for certain that she and Warwick had been lovers. There was nothing wrong with that; most girls had lovers before they finally met the right guy. And surely she cared only for him. He knew women too well to be deceived for such a long time. And they could work out the past. She could explain that to him. And she would be with him during the coming ordeal. She would help share the burden.

Once again he tried to close his eyes and find the refuge of sleep, but again the demons of guilt began their work. He wished he had a pill, a powerful drug, to force him to sleep. Anything to give him release, not just from the fatigue, but also from the pain. His eyes wandered relentlessly around the soft, luxurious space. How strange that now, his most despairing moment, he should be encapsulated in such luxury and comfort—a first-class cabin. Those were the rewards for effort and goodness, not for what he had done. For the first time in his life he was relieved his father was dead. Never could he have explained what had happened. Never could he have faced the big, watery blue eyes which saw everything, understood everything. For the judgment would have been inescapable, and the retribution unbearable.

With that thought he knew he had to stand and walk around. He carefully stepped over Irene and made his way toward the cabin's kitchen. A pert young Swiss girl stood sleepily and asked if he wanted something. He asked for a whiskey with ice and waited patiently while she found the plastic glass and tiny bottles. She poured two of them, probably so she wouldn't be bothered for another. Richard took the glass and drank half of it. He had never really liked bourbon, but perhaps it would help him to sleep. It was the least of the sins his father would have noticed, although it was a sign of cowardice.

He took the glass and returned to his seat. Irene was still asleep, but her blanket had fallen. He replaced the blanket tenderly and sat down. Warwick was reclined in the seat across the aisle, his long legs stretched out in front of him and his mouth agape. He was obviously deeply asleep, and apparently carrying no great burden with him into that defenseless realm. Was it that he had no conscience? Or that his inner powers allowed him respite from such cares? Richard looked at the face—smooth and clear, despite the hint of beard on his jaw. It was the face of privilege, with none of the scars and flaws that marked youth as he had known it. Even the eyelids were soft and rounded, as if a mark of caste—of right. Warwick's shoulders twitched suddenly, a quick, shiverlike spasm. Perhaps he was cold or physically worn. Perhaps it was a touch of torment— the awful intruder's first tapping at the gate. But Richard knew one thing as he looked at the seeming innocence and peacefulness of Warwick's face. His relationship with him would never be the same. Never. He had shown he would put his own interests paramount to Richard's, whatever the cost. And he knew Warwick was fighting for his life, and he would stop at nothing. Richard wanted to hate him, but didn't have the will.

Finally drowsiness swept over him and his head fell gradually toward his chest. He felt himself opiated, his consciousness falling rapidly toward a point behind his

178

eyes. He knew relief was arriving, and he would find peace. He descended gratefully into the blackness, everything turning soft and safe. There would be a solution with the dawn. He would be happy once again.

But while asleep he dreamed, vivid dreams in bright, garish colors and angry muffled sounds. There was an endless cotton field, with row after row of huge, overgrown plants, swaying and twisting in anxiety. In the distance, Warwick sat astride a giant tractor—its roar wafting in and out—reaping the plants with giant, flashing blades. And the nearer the tractor came, the more fervidly the plants writhed, their squares becoming sticky and bursting, and spewing out helpless, sickly strands of unborn cotton which spilled to the ground where they wiggled and became soiled.

Richard jerked awake, relieved to be alive and away from the dream. But as he cleared his eyes and looked around the soft blue and gray cabin, he remembered where he was and the circumstances in which he was caught. He quietly opened the window cover next to his seat and looked out into the dull, gray nothingness. The plane was descending. He felt as if it were floating gently. The stewardesses were busy in the kitchen, and two passengers were lined up in front of the toilet.

He now knew that things were really going to happen and mused how different reality was from his earlier expectations of Switzerland. What was supposed to have been an exciting, playful adventure would, he feared, turn into an encounter with strange and hostile persons and events. He felt so empty, so defenseless, and depression blotted out all joy of and fascination with the newness of what was about to happen.

Gracefully the plane glided under the last of the clouds and corrected itself for the landing in Zurich. Richard strained toward the window; even though exhausted, he was awed by the majestic mountains and neat, picture-book farms below. They touched down perfectly and came to a gentle halt. He woke Irene and helped her retrieve her coat and hand luggage. Finally they all stood and filed out the doorway onto buses. The comfort and protection of the first-class cabin were gone; they were now part of the rest of the world, with its frailties and insecurities.

At the arrival gate they saw Swiss paratroopers lugging mammoth machine guns slung by straps from their shoulders. "Damn!" Richard gasped. "There must be something going on."

"No, no," an older Swiss next to him replied. "That's simply a precaution against terrorists. They're instructed to shoot before asking questions."

Richard stole a quizzical glance at Warwick and mouthed the word "gun." "In the suitcase, stupid," he whispered. Richard had always read how peaceful the Swiss were as a nation. He now knew that was simply another in a long line of misconceptions.

The luggage arrived promptly, and the four, indicating they had nothing to declare, walked through the customs

180

door. Once outside, Warwick instructed the taxi driver to take them to the Hilton near the airport. "You and Sammie register for three rooms," Warwick told Richard softly. "I'm going to stay out of the way."

Warwick browsed in the gift shop while Richard registered at the desk. He volunteered the passports of Irene and Sammie. He planned to answer that he had forgotten about Warwick, in the event the desk clerk should ask for his passport, but he didn't ask. Richard walked into the gift shop and bought a newspaper. "Six-twenty," he mumbled to Warwick, then left. The ride up the elevator was slow. Irene leaned against Richard, already half asleep. Sammie leaned against one of the walls, his eyes closed. The man seemed to have no emotion, Richard noticed. He held all his cards behind his back.

The suite was simple, yet tasteful. Richard tipped the bellman, then proceeded with Irene toward the bedroom. She immediately fell on the bed and curled up to sleep. Richard placed a blanket over her and began to undress. He turned on the shower and stepped inside. The hot steamy water was the most familiar thing he had felt for hours, and it relaxed him. The large, soft towel felt good, as he dried himself before the mirror. He noticed he needed a shave, so returned to the bedroom to open the luggage. Warwick was sitting in one of the soft chairs, staring at him.

"We have an appointment at the bank in about an hour," he said. "Wear a suit—look like a successful young businessman. It'll only take a few minutes, then it's all over."

Neither spoke during the twenty-five-minute ride from the hotel to the Bahnhofstrasse in the center of the city. Warwick leaned against his door of the taxi, staring at the back of the driver's seat and biting his lower lip. Richard looked out the opposite window, terribly worn by the travel, his eyes beginning to play tricks. The city had become fogbound, and everything seemed gray or close to gray. There was no snow, but the parks were bare, and the pedestrians hid their faces as they shuffled swiftly along the sidewalks. The city was disorienting; the buildings were all the same height, and Richard couldn't decide whether they were headed toward the center of the city or were simply making circles.

At one point he had again started to tell Warwick he wouldn't go through with the transaction. But Warwick had reasoned in the lobby that accepting a cash delivery was in the ordinary course of their business; it was something they did in commodities all the time. If, by some chance, they should have difficulties with creditors, the money would simply be another asset they could attach. Richard had found the argument convincing, but he also knew Warwick would want to hide the money. He raised his hands and messaged his eyes deeply. He was so tired, tired more from the anxiety than from the trip. But he accepted Warwick's argument that simply taking the money wouldn't be a crime, and it gave everyone time.

The taxi came to a halt in front of a large stone building with the name of the bank over the entrance. Warwick reached in his pocket wearily and paid the driver. They both stepped out and straightened their clothes. "This is all you need," Warwick said, handing him a Manila envelope. "It's all the delivery documents. I'll wait in that cafe across the street. Just come over for a drink when you're finished."

Richard turned and started to walk inside. He stopped abruptly and yelled to Warwick crossing the street. "Who do I see?" he asked.

"Herr Falez!" Warwick shouted in response. "Second floor!"

With that, they both turned and proceeded.

Inside there was a small, sparse lobby, quite unlike the banks at home. Richard asked a guard for the office of Herr Falez and was directed toward an elevator. He rode the tiny elevator to the second floor and stepped out. A young receptionist took his name and made a call. She then led him down a long, plain hallway to a private room. She told him Herr Falez would be there shortly, and asked if he wanted a cup of coffee. He shook his head and took off his coat.

Almost immediately a small middle-aged man, wearing a gray tweed suit, walked through another door. Richard extended his hand and said, "How are you? I'm Richard Johnson."

"Falez—good day," the man answered quietly, offering

Richard a seat. "Did you bring the receipts, Mr. Johnson?"

"Yes, I did," Richard answered, fumbling with the envelope. "Everything's in here."

"Let me see," Herr Falez mumbled, pulling the documents from the envelope. "I . . . don't think you have endorsed them."

Richard waited while the Swiss checked for the correct spaces on which to endorse the receipts, then took a proffered pen and signed where instructed. He knew it was foolish to sign a document without reading it, but he had done so many things foolishly lately, what was another? "I'll be back in a moment," Herr Falez said, his eyes looking at Richard's face for the first time. "Would you like a cup of coffee?"

"No, thank you," Richard answered.

"One moment," the banker repeated, before leaving quietly.

Richard looked around the room. The walls were covered with an off-white wallpaper with thin blue lines. Sheer curtains covered inset windows. There was a large, simple Paul Klee print on one wall. No magazines were on the tables. The room felt like a prison cell to Richard, so he closed his eyes to relieve the claustrophobia. Shortly, the door opened again.

"I forgot to ask for your passport," Herr Falez stated. Richard found it in his coat pocket and handed it to him. "I'll return shortly," he said.

Again Richard closed his eyes, and his mind began to wander. Suppose they had been alerted? he asked himself, and his eyes popped open. But how could they? It's Warwick's name that's being talked about, not mine. His anxiety increased, and he decided to stand. Just then the door opened. Falez and another man entered.

"Two or three more things to sign, Mr. Johnson, and everything will be in order," Herr Falez said, taking a seat.

Richard signed several more documents in both English and German. "These are mere formalities," the Swiss murmured.

Richard finished signing, and the other man, Herr Seiler, folded the documents and stood. "The money will be in the account tomorrow," he said. "I hope that's not an inconvenience?"

"Why, of course, not," Richard answered casually. He had to presume it wasn't.

Richard shook hands with both men and turned toward the door. When outside the entrance, he inhaled deeply, drinking in the cold, clean air. That much was over, and he would have a few hours, at least, to figure out what to do next. He carefully crossed the Bahnhofstrasse, dodging a streetcar whirring past. He walked through the revolving door of the cafe and looked around. Warwick was seated at a table near the window, grinning broadly.

"We did it, ol' boy!" Warwick shouted over the heads of the other patrons. "We did it!"

Richard was glad to see Warwick smile again. Maybe

185

things would turn normal for a while. Just maybe everything was going to turn out all right.

"Now we're going skiin'," Warwick announced, offering Richard a seat. "I've got us a villa in Zermatt. It'll only take two or three hours to get there, then we can relax and have a little fun."

"The money won't be in the account until tomorrow," Richard said, watching the waiter place a beer in front of him.

"I know," Warwick replied. "But don't worry. It's a numbered account I had 'em set up for me a while ago. Meanwhile you can go skiin' with Sammie—he's a devil on skis."

Warwick drove the big Mercedes, with Sammie alongside; Richard and Irene sat curled up in the back seat. Dusk was descending swiftly, as they floated through the Swiss countryside. The architecture and dress were different and fascinating to Richard; even the advertisements were discreet and tucked away. Irene had had a few hours of sleep, but then had dressed and bought food for the trip. After they had eaten the tasty sausages and rolls and various salads, she put everything away and again fell asleep. It felt good holding her in his lap. It gave him a sense of strength and purpose. But gnawing doubts about her feelings toward Warwick returned. He was bothered not so much about the intimacies between her and Warwick as about the emotional bonds. Could those ever be broken, if they were as strong as Warwick had said?

The gray drifted toward black, the lights from on-coming automobiles glaring rudely. The Mercedes sped further and further into the darkness, hurtling itself smoothly toward a future as new and unknown as the night itself. But Richard was too tired to let those fears disturb him. Gently he shifted Irene and stretched his legs across the back seat, leaning his head against her purse. There would be a few days of respite before he would have to make any more decisions. And surely prospects would turn better. His eyelids shut as if weighted, and as he drifted off he fretted for no reason at all about skiing with Sammie.

17

THE DAZZLING LIGHT streaming through the window finally stirred Richard from his sleep. He propped himself on one elbow and looked out the large windows toward the majestic Matterhorn in the distance. Tiny sparkling ice motes danced playfully in the crystal-clear sunlight. His head was light and clear, and his body felt rested. Gone was the heaviness of depression and care. He felt cleansed, almost buoyant. He leaned back on the enormous down pillow and let his body stretch and tingle. It felt good to be alive—and no longer afraid.

Irene lay next to him, her glistening hair spilled across the pillow. Slowly he reached with his hand under the puffy cover and caressed the suedelike skin on her shoulders and back and buttocks. His hand probed further, until she awoke gently. He then leaned over her and kissed her still sleepy face, his body moving closer and then next to her own. They slowly embraced and began caressing each other soundlessly, until finally they united. Then began a slow and rhythmical mating that seemed to pass without time or place, reaching gradually an ecstatic and blinding finale in which their pleasure became limitless and universal. Then they lay entwined, staring at the clean white walls and ceiling, enjoying the warmth of the rays from the sun. It was for them a most contented moment.

Eventually Sammie knocked roughly on the door to announce breakfast was ready. Richard leaped from the bed and headed toward the bathroom.

"What time is it?" Irene asked with a yawn.

"Look at my watch on the table," Richard yelled from the bathroom.

"It's only eight o'clock," she shouted lazily. "Why don't we stay in bed?"

"I want to go skiing," Richard answered.

"We can do that this afternoon," she pouted, pulling the covers over her shoulders.

"I want to go this morning," Richard mumbled through a toothbrush at the door. "It's a great day outside."

"Well, I'm going to stay here," she answered, pulling the covers over her head.

"Suit yourself, lazy," Richard answered, returning to the bathroom and sitting on the side of the enormous porcelain tub.

"I will," he heard her reply, as rusty water gushed blood red from the steamy faucet.

The villa was built around a huge central room which reached to the rafters. On one wall, two-storied windows looked out toward the mountains. The three other walls supported second-story balconies. A gigantic stone fireplace dominated a seating area filled with leather couches and animal-skin rugs and heavily carved furniture. At night the room was warm and inviting, light from the fire flickering into shadowy corners. But during the day the sun bleached out the romance, and most visitors spent their mornings in the breakfast room at one end of the large, cheerful kitchen.

As Richard entered the kitchen, he saw Sammie standing before a large gas stove, preparing eggs and bacon on the griddle. Warwick was seated at an oak table in the breakfast area, reading a newspaper. "What's going on in New York?" Richard asked, stealing a piece of bacon from Sammie's platter.

"I don't think you want to know," Warwick muttered, lifting his coffee cup. "It's about what we expected."

"Well, how bad is it?" Richard asked, taking a seat.

"Cotton's still locked the limit," he replied, brushing a crumb from his plaid ski sweater. "I'd just as soon not talk about it."

"I wanna ski the glacier," Sammie announced, while stirring the scrambled eggs. "Who's got the balls to come with me?"

"What the hell's the 'glacier'?" Richard asked, draining the last of his orange juice.

"You go up to the top of the lifts and then hike a little bit," Sammie replied. "There's an ice glacier up there. You can ski and cross-country all the way to Italy—catch a lift back from there."

"Sounds great," Richard answered. "You coming, War?"

190

"Naw. I've got a few errands to run. I'll take a short run this afternoon."

The three ate leisurely, then Richard and Sammie left for the center of town. Richard was glad to be able to spend a whole day with Sammie; maybe it would improve their relationship. They rented good equipment and supplies at a swank shop on the main street, then walked to the lift, where they bought tickets and received instructions. They boarded one of the gondolas and began their ascent.

The day was becoming warmer, and bright sunshine flooded the beautiful valley and its fresh snow. Richard was exhilarated, his eyes feasted on the scenery and the other skiers. Everything was so comfortable and well organized, nothing like the rugged ski trips when he was in school and penniless. Sammie was quiet as usual, but Richard noticed something strange. Whenever the gondola would swing or lurch, Sammie's hands would grip the supports, his face turning grim and white. He must really like to ski, Richard thought to himself, if he's that afraid of heights.

At the last stop they disembarked and asked an instructor the directions toward the glacier. He gave them detailed instructions and warned them to stay on the marked trail. It was easy to get lost, he explained, and there were large cracks in the ice. He then told them how to make the return trip by lift from Italy.

The climb to the starting point was strenuous, and Sammie had to stop several times to rest. He found it difficult to breathe in the thin air, and his boots were making his feet sore. After about an hour, they reached their destination and prepared to ski. Richard helped Sammie with his bindings, then affixed his own. Sammie was even more silent than usual; he was obviously very uncomfortable in the high altitude.

"You sure you want to do this?" Richard asked.

"Yep," was the reply.

With a nod of heads, they began their descent down the other side of the mountain. The snow was fresh and light, and slipping down the gentle terrain was like flying. Richard led the way, while Sammie worked to keep up. They came to the first marker, and Richard stopped to be sure Sammie was all right.

"Look at the view, will ya" Richard exclaimed, whipping off his sunglasses. "Not a human being in sight. Just mountains and snow and air!"

"Yeah, looks great," Sammie replied between deep breaths. "Let's move on."

So they shoved off again, across a dazzling plain; this time Richard made wide sweeps in the snow to make it easier for Sammie. Richard became almost adolescent in his exuberance, jumping and swooping playfully. It was skiing as he had never experienced it before. After thirty minutes more they came to a halt near a marker and agreed to have lunch. They each produced box lunches, which they had bought at the ski shop, and sat down to enjoy the fresh sausages and cheese. There were even small cans of beer, which they shoved into the snow. Three other skiers swept past them and waved.

192

"This is where we turn," Sammie announced, unfolding the map and inspecting the marker.

"No, no," Richard replied. "We're supposed to stay on the dark line. The patrol fellow said we should always keep that mountain in front of us."

"Well, I ran into a Swiss guy last night in one of the saloons," Sammie countered. "And he said to take the dotted line. He said it's much more interesting—the snow's deeper."

"Well, if you say so," Richard replied.

"Hell, you only do it once," Sammie growled with a grin. "If it scares ya—"

"Hell, no," Richard retorted, draining the last of his beer. "This'll be a piece of cake."

Once again they shoved off, Richard spraying snow from side to side in short, quick turns. Sammie doggedly maintained the pace, his shoulders hunched and skis wide. Sammie seemed to thrive on the challenge, Richard noticed. Otherwise, how could he enjoy such effort? The terrain became gradually steeper and the snow icier, but the two continued their journey. Finally the ominous, cold shadow of one of the mountains fell across the trail, and they could feel the temperature fall rapidly.

"I guess we've got to go on," Richard said, himself panting from the work and the thin air. "We sure can't climb back up the mountain."

Sammie's face glistened with sweat, his wool-stocking cap damp against the skin. He didn't speak, but instead nodded his head with determination. So again they let fly, speeding nonstop for a quarter of a mile, until they came to a narrow tree line. It would be difficult navigating through the forest; the snow was deep. and the trees were dense.

"Hey, let's take a break," Sammie gasped.

"Sure," Richard answered, his own legs beginning to feel the strain.

Richard leaned his poles against one of the trees and bent over to adjust a binding. He was aware that Sammie was struggling with the zipper on his jacket, but it wasn't until he heard the grunts that he looked up. Sammie had opened the jacket and was pulling something from under his sweater. He had grasped it, but it was hung on the threads. He was absurdly frustrated, his eyes wide and animal gasps spitting from his mouth. It was a pistol. It looked like a .45, and an adjustment on the end was snared by the wool. It looked like a choke, or a silencer, which Richard had seen in the movies. He started to ask if he could help.

"Say, put that away!" Richard whispered, staring at the handle. "They'll put your ass in jail for that. They're real strict on foreigners with guns here."

Sammie tore violently at the sweater, his hand shaking and his face contorted with effort.

"What the hell are you doing?" Richard asked, taking the ski poles in his hands.

Again there was no reply. Sammie finally tore through the sweater and began extricating the gun's sight from strands of wool. But it was something from another plane of life which caused Richard to move, something certainly beyond reason or consciousness—something compelled by the look on Sammie's face. Richard hadn't traveled ten yards when a huge chunk exploded from the bark of an evergreen next to his shoulder.

With that, Richard jabbed his poles into the snow and jammed his legs against the skis, fighting, fighting to create distance. It was mostly instinctual or perhaps something he had learned as a boy hunting squirrels and rabbits. His whole being told him to strain every muscle, every sense, to make distance, to escape. Faster and faster he dodged between the trees—any one of which could have proved, at that speed, an absolute barrier. But he pushed and pushed, as never before, knowing this race was different from any other in his life. Everything within told him to flee—to *flee*.

Suddenly Richard lost his balance and fell face forward down the steep incline. When the slide finally ceased, he was stunned. His leg stretched awkwardly behind him, the boot free from its binding. He looked back hurriedly. Though seeing nothing, he heard the labored efforts of Sammie's movements. In panic, he pulled himself erect, wincing at the numbed pain from his knee. He knew it was damaged, but also knew that was now secondary. He bent over to affix the binding with his hands, his eyes riveted through the trees. He glimpsed Sammie's red jacket perhaps fifteen yards away.

Then he saw Sammie stop and lift the grotesque weapon. Again, Richard shoved deeply against the snow, his hands pushing against the bark of a tree. The snow at his feet exploded. With a pathetic whine, he strove again, knowing he must flee, must outrun the evil. The leg was hurt, but that didn't matter. Nothing mattered, except to escape. He skied blindly, pleading with himself to maintain control, not to lose control.

Twenty yards farther he stopped, his head moving from side to side. How could he escape? His tracks were so perfectly clear. And his knee was so weak, he knew it could fold at any time, regardless of how well he endured the pain. But he continued the run, weaving as best he could between giant tree trunks, praying an impossible turn would not suddenly appear. Then again he went sprawling, this time losing both skis. His face was buried downhill in the pristine snow.

Slowly and painfully he pulled himself erect, awkwardly replacing the skis. Was there any use? Was there any escape from the mighty weapon? He heard Sammie approaching through the trees, his skis crunching against the snow arrhythmically. Richard tried to hold the huge billows of breath coming out his mouth; surely they would give him away. But then he remembered the tracks he had left. They were immutable. And Sammie came nearer and nearer, his own breathing becoming audible in the silence of the forest. There was nothing between them but the staid, disinterested trees. What would he do? How could he get away?

Then all became silent. Not even the wind stirred. Richard waited. He knew that death was present.

196

"Come on out!" Sammie shouted hoarsely. "Get your butt out here!"

Richard said nothing, instinct telling him that speaking would do no good. He heard Sammie move a few feet closer—he would have trouble aiming the pistol while sliding. Again a tree just behind him exploded, showering fresh chips on the snow. A half foot wide hole gaped blindly.

"If you don't come out, *I'm goin' to make it hurt!*" Sammie screamed, as if out of control.

Richard started to speak, to plead, but again stopped himself. He looked at the wound in the tree and wondered what such force would do to flesh. His eyes turned dark for an instant. Don't lose control! Don't lose control!

He heard Sammie again move toward the tree. Should he run while Sammie was off balance? Should he say something? At least ask *why?* He heard Sammie coming closer and closer. He had to do something. He reached over his head for a dead branch. Perhaps it would break. Perhaps he would have some defense against the grotesque power of the pistol. As he grabbed the branch an avalanche of snow fell from the heavy branches overhead. At first Richard was blinded, but then he heard Sammie cursing wildly—he had fallen down with the impact. By reflex, Richard turned and slid farther down the hill, gambling that Sammie couldn't fire for a few seconds, and praying those few seconds would put a merciful distance between them—even if just temporarily. He favored the bad knee. If it went out, all was over.

"You might as well stop!" he heard Sammie scream. "I'm gonna get ya! You got my best friend all fucked up. You cost my sister her whole life. You're a *dog*, bastard, and you're gonna die like one! You came between me and my family, son-of-a-bitch! You're gonna *die!*"

And so the two skiers, the hunter and the hunted, made their way slowly through the forest. Richard took what precautions he could to protect his knee, while moving so as to keep the trees between himself and Sammie. Occasionally, without warning, savage damage would befall things around him. Time was running out. It would take only one of those blasts to end his life. One thing only commanded his consciousness—survival. For ten seconds, a minute, perhaps. Survival, the central government of us all.

A hundred yards later, Richard caught sight of the end of the tree line. There the glacier returned, with a frightening angle of descent and a limitless, cold openness. He kept moving—he couldn't stop—with every sense and intelligence concentrated on this new obstacle. He would have to ski out in the open, at threatening speed. The knee would surely buckle; he could hardly withstand the pain as it was. The ligaments were probably torn—certainly weakened to the verge. He reached the last tree and clung to it for support. This was it—turn back and plead with the madman or attempt the suicidal. He squinted down the glistening slope. He had lost his sunglasses and couldn't even ascertain the contour. What to do? What to do? He suddenly heard Sammie's skis, only a few yards away.

With that he entered a slow and painful crouch, wrapping his arms around his knees. He paused for a second and rubbed the bad one, as if to plead with it. And then he threw away his poles. He wondered briefly if that was a mistake. And then he took a deep gulp of air and began sliding, his head atop his knees; he could feel the texture of the tight, fashionable fabric.

The slide seemed so slow, he could even see the little rivulets of crystal on the ice. At that pace, he would be nothing but an easy target for the massive gun. His whole back and head were exposed—maybe the pain would be brief, the results instant. But he slid and slid, yet it seemed so slow. It wasn't going to work, but it was the only thing left in life. And then he felt himself accelerating, the terrain bumping him roughly, and the wind tearing his eyes. He had no thought of what was in front of him or where he was going. He knew only that he had to put space between himself and death. Faster and faster, he sped more dangerously than ever in his life. But it was working. He was gaining life, he thought.

Until he saw, at the last possible second, the yawning fissure beneath him. He didn't really know that his legs were stretching out, flexing as never before, and that he was sailing through the gentle air. For it was all over. There was no more meaning—only the slight sensation of wind.

When he hit the snow, he felt his face crush into the raw ice beneath. And, for some reason—perhaps to avoid the irritation—he tucked a shoulder and allowed himself to slide for a time. He stopped against a mogul, but was there awhile before he realized he was motionless. Lying there, he stared blindly at the enormous azure sky; he felt tired in the shoulders and was glad to have the respite. The snow next to him then exploded into a dazzling fountain of white matter.

His reflex was so violent, he could feel his shoulders ache as he scrambled on all fours over the mogul and then sideways to hide himself. The hunt was still on, and he had lost his skis. He quickly turned to see if he could walk or run or slide any farther. The glacier flattened out from that point into a vast, clear plain. It was hopeless without skis, and those were lost in sight of the hunter. He then heard a voice.

"If ya quit runnin', we can talk about it!" Sammie yelled from the tree line, his voice carrying clear and precise across the emptiness.

Again instinct told Richard the offer had no value, not after the previous blasts.

"If ya don't quit, I'm gonna come after ya," Sammie yelled again. "Ya ain't got your skis. I can see 'em. So just stand up and climb on back!"

Richard lay silent, caressing the snow with his cheek, back and forth, as would an infant his mother's skin. And then nothing happened. Time passed. There was no sound. No movement. He waited. He had no shelter, no alternative. He was trapped. His leg was hurt and he had lost his skis. He was trapped. Nothing else remained, except the waiting. His eyes darted against the snow.

And then he heard the dreaded sound. Sammie was descending the hill. He was snowplowing down the glacier, bearing sure, imminent death. Richard dug his face farther into the snow. He wanted to cry, but his senses overpowered his emotions. And that's when he heard the awkward sounds. One in particular seemed hideous— *"Uph!"* And then he heard more sounds—a cacophony of scratchings and scrapes and slides. He looked up to see Sammie sliding out of control, apparently not worried, the pistol held high. Farther and farther down the steep ice he slid, his speed increasing more and more. And then he must have seen the terrible chasm, the open grave, for his body sprang up with a mighty thrust, a monumental defiance. But still no sounds—perhaps out of disbelief—as he raced nearer and nearer. Until, without a whisper, he disappeared into the earth.

Richard lay braced against the snow. It had happened so fast. He had never seen a man die. But Sammie was dead, and all that he had meant. And Richard was alive. He fell again into the embrace of the snow and lay there awhile, as though in a dream. But then he felt a shiver and shook himself. He pulled himself slowly across the mogul to where his skis lay scattered. He cleaned them carefully, tenderly, then began fastening them onto his feet. He was so tired, so very tired, but he knew he could make it to the village at the bottom of the glacier. He raised himself slowly and looked toward the bottom of the valley. It would be a long trip with a game leg, but he knew he could do it. And it would be a pleasure. He had survived.

18

THE CAFE WAS stuffy, its windows steamed. The crowd of skiers didn't seem to mind, their faces glistening as they drank and conversed boisterously. Richard sat at the end of a long wooden table cupping a mug of hot chocolate. He was sore and terribly tired, but relieved to be around such secure people, even though they didn't know the truth. A pretty girl with cropped black hair leaned over and asked a question in Italian. As Richard looked up, she repeated the question in French. He simply looked at her, wondering if she had ever seen death, wondering if she were a nurse or had ever worked in a hospital. She shrugged her shoulders and smiled. Then several of her companions took seats around him, jostling and joking in German. He moved his stool farther toward the window, then realized there weren't enough seats. He decided to stand, but the group protested. He smiled to assure them he had to leave; the lift back to Zermatt would soon cease operation. The thought of the cool, fresh air outside frightened him.

More skiers pushed inside, as he politely threaded his way out. They all seemed so confident and cheerful. They had never been through what he had experienced. They had all led such normal lives, which meant that his was twisted and miscreant. The air was refreshing, even though it brought back memories of the events of the day. They would go away, he told himself; there's no fault with nature, with the elements.

Richard limped painfully from the cafe toward the lift station. People ran every which way, each seeming to know exactly where he was going. Richard knew he had to return to Zermatt. Everything was there—his money, his clothes... her. What other choice was there? He had nothing. He followed the line to the door of the gondola, stacked his skis, and stepped aboard. Richard knew he was headed toward the villa, and toward a world completely different from the one he had left in the morning. Sammie had tried to murder him, and he was now dead. He was the brother of Irene, and the close friend of Warwick. Maybe Sammie was simply crazy; he had shouted insanities about his sister and Warwick. But that alone wouldn't cause someone to murder. It seemed too planned, too available, to have been done impulsively.

The big, warm gondola slowly lifted away from the village, then accelerated along its smooth, sure path toward Switzerland. Richard leaned against the window, the pride of survival reviving inside. But his eyes felt leaden, rolling back and drawing him toward release. He had so many things to consider, so many things to decide. The gondola hummed and swayed, and his aching body relaxed by inches into the seat. He knew what lay ahead was critical, but his body surrendered. There was nothing but the humming of the cables and the gentle, kind protection of the interior.

Richard jerked awake, as the last of the passengers left the lift. Drowsily he pulled himself erect and stumbled out the door. It had turned dark, which added to his feeling of loneliness and isolation. He removed his skis and hoisted them to his shoulder. He suddenly remembered the operator in Italy hadn't punched his ticket. A sense of guilt overwhelmed him. Everyone was expected to be honest in Switzerland. Once again he had transgressed.

Groups of vacationers walked past arm in arm, laughing and jostling playfully. Richard remembered when life for him was so carefree, and wondered if it would ever be so again. Once he had his share of the money, he knew things would be much better. He could pay off his debts, at least, which would give him the courage to face the other consequences upon his return to Memphis. But he dreaded desperately returning to the villa. He no longer knew who Irene truly was, and certainly knew he could never trust Warwick again. But maybe they weren't involved with Sammie; maybe it was simply his own perversity. But then what would he say to Irene—your brother died trying to kill me; I watched him die and let him die. And would there be further danger? If Warwick was behind Sammie, would he try something himself? He too had a weapon—the .38.

Slowly he trudged along the neatly cleared paths toward the villa. His knee had swelled during the trip back and was even more painful. But he knew a hot bath would help, followed by an ice pack. Suddenly the great stone house loomed ahead. He paused, again to decide whether to return. He had to; he had to play the charade. But he would take no chances. Warwick surely wouldn't try anything in the house. But if he did, Richard knew one thing—he would kill Warwick in self-defense.

The heavy carved door was unlocked, so he pushed it open. In the vestibule he placed his skis in a rack and removed his boots. He had forgotten how sore his feet were, so he rubbed them tenderly. He pushed through the interior door and felt a rush of warm air. He fumbled for a light switch and flipped it on. Immediately the huge living room lighted up. There was no sign of life. Even the fire was out. "Anyone home?" he shouted. There was nothing but silence.

Richard slowly mounted the stairs, hopping on his good leg to protect the other. He reached the bedroom he shared with Irene, and looked down the hall toward Warwick's. The door was shut and the lights out. He opened the door to his room and turned on the light. The bed had been made, and his suitcase and Irene's lay on top of it, their things neatly packed inside. Why would she have done that? They were supposed to stay a week in the mountains. Then he turned and padded down the hallway to Warwick's room. Should he knock? Perhaps they were there together, locked in their seamy conspiracy. He grabbed the handle and flung the door wide.

There was nothing, only darkness. He turned on the

light and looked around the room. It was in disarray, as Warwick's bedroom always was. The bed covers were clumsily pulled up, and clothes and personal items were strewn about haphazardly. Why am I doing this? Richard asked himself. I should leave this room. But he knew he wanted to know if there was any sign, any message of betrayal.

He walked to the bed and flung back the covers. They were clean; no refuse of pleasure, no dull browns or yellows. He then turned and looked further. Warwick's leather briefcase lay opened atop the desk. Richard walked toward it, wondering what it would mean to him. He picked up the folder on top and opened it. Inside were papers from the bank—account numbers, instructions for withdrawal and transfer of funds. Underneath lay a large Manila envelope marked "Sammie." It was sealed, but he tore it open anyway. That was his right; he had the right to know what was inside. It was crisp, new U.S. currency— there must have been about fifty thousand dollars. Richard stood stunned; there had to be a connection. If Warwick had owed Sammie the money, he would have given it to him by now. This money must have been for something else, something conditional. At least he knew the value of his own life—fifty thousand dollars. He stuffed the envelope in his ski jacket and probed further. He found the heavy black .38 in a tooled leather case. He remembered holding a .38 one time back home. The sheriff's deputy demonstrated its awesome power one afternoon by shooting turtles in the creek that ran by the school. It was short and snub-nosed, a characteristic which reduced its accuracy, except at close range. It was a weapon designed to maim and kill; it had no other virtue. Richard slipped it also into the ski jacket; that would eliminate one risk.

The other items in the briefcase were valueless—passport, airline tickets, datebook, *Playboy* magazine. Richard thought about the passport; taking that would surely twist the bastard's knickers. But it would also interfere with getting the money, and that was the key. He left everything else as it was and shuffled down the hall to his room.

There he again saw the suitcases. Why shouldn't he finish packing and simply run, he asked himself. That would be so simple, so safe. He had the fifty thousand—his blood money—but that was not enough to cover the debts. No, he would stay. He would stage a little drama for Warwick. He quickly left the room and made his way toward the other side of the house. Sammie's bags too were packed, except for a few valuables lying atop the dresser. He picked them up and dropped them in one of the suitcases. He then picked everything up and returned to the hall. There he saw a staircase leading to the top floor. He climbed it slowly, using one of the suitcases as a crutch. At the top everything was dark, so he groped his way along until he found an open door and flicked on the light.

It was another bedroom, only smaller, with a whole wall of linen closets. He opened one of them and removed several blankets. He shoved Sammie's luggage inside and covered it with the blankets. "Goodbye, asshole," he mumbled to himself. He then made his way down the stairs and toward his room. He smiled to himself; let Warwick do a little guessing for a while, a little tit for tat.

He undressed and limped into the bathroom. He started the water in the giant tub and sat on the toilet to inspect his knee. It was swollen and turning blue. It was worse than anything he had had while running track. But then his mind's eye saw the suddenly chewed-up trees and the spewing snow. What the hell was a bum knee? he thought, his hand sweeping over his stomach and shoulders. A vision of his body mutilated by one of those bullets appeared, and he hung his head between his knees. Suddenly sounds came from below.

They had returned. Richard could hear Warwick and Irene talking about logs for the fire. Richard moved quietly into the bedroom, removing the money, folder, and pistol from his ski jacket. He placed the money in a toiletries kit and the pistol in the toe of a cowboy boot. He shoved the folder into the bottom of his suitcase. He then pulled his robe from the luggage and left the room. The voices became clearer as he approached the balcony and stairs. He thought of eavesdropping, but instinct told him to carry through with his subterfuge. As he limped down the stairs, he shouted, "Where the hell you guys been? I'm hungry as hell."

Warwick wheeled around from the fireplace, his mouth

open and face ashen. He said nothing, but followed Richard intensely with his eyes, as he descended the last of the steps.

"Hurt my knee coming down," Richard grimaced, limping into the room. "But it was a hell of a lot of fun."

Warwick continued to stare, holding a piece of newspaper awkwardly in front of him.

"What did you all do?" Richard asked, sliding onto one of the couches. "Get up on the slopes?"

Warwick still didn't speak, or move. He continued staring at Richard, until finally he lowered his arm. "We . . . we went shopping," he answered.

Irene walked into the room and saw Richard. She smiled and said, "Oh, I thought you two were going to spend the night in Italy. What happened?"

"Sammie didn't want to go," Richard answered, stretching out on the couch. "He said altitudes make him sick. So he went off to one of the lower runs, and I went on by myself."

Warwick hadn't moved, his hand still holding the newspaper.

"He should be back by now," Irene said quietly, taking one of the easy chairs. "He probably met some girl."

"I could sure stand a drink," Richard told Irene. "I hurt the hell out of my knee—do you mind?"

Irene nodded and hopped from her chair. He watched her hair swing as she made her way to the kitchen.

"Sammie's the one who wanted to ski the glacier," Warwick said quietly. "He's the one who organized it."

"Yeah, but he changed his mind," Richard answered, placing his hand behind his neck. "But he sold me on it, and I went ahead with some other guys. Great stuff, War. You ought to try it."

Without speaking, Warwick walked toward the stairs, ascended them two at a time, and hastened toward his room. Irene returned with a glass of whiskey. She handed it to Richard and sat down beside him.

"Hurt my knee," he said, taking a long pull from the drink.

"How?" she asked, lifting the robe.

"Hell of a fall," he answered, looking at her eyes for signs.

"Oooh, poor baby," she sighed, touching the knee. "You need to soak it."

"Got anything to eat?" Richard asked. "All they gave me was a roll and sausage."

"I'll see what's there," she answered, rising and walking toward the kitchen. "I think there's a minute steak in the ice box."

His thoughts raced. He saw live signs in Warwick. She was something else; she revealed nothing. But Sammie had yelled he had come between them. What did that mean? Was she in league with Warwick? Was she party to the conspiracy?

Warwick appeared at the top of the stairs. "Where's Sammie?" he demanded coldly.

"Probably out chasin' puss," Richard answered, taking another long sip from his drink. "What's the matter?"

"Don't you know?" Warwick asked.

"Know what?" Richard replied, leaning on his side. "Boy, a fire sure would feel good."

"That *bastard!*" Warwick shouted, his head held back with his eyes closed.

"What's that?" Richard asked, feeling comfortable with his performance.

"That *cocksucker!*" Warwick roared, striking his fist into the other hand.

"What's the matter?" Richard asked.

"He's split," Warwick answered with disappointment. "The fucker's ... *split!*"

"You mean Sammie?" Richard asked.

"Hell, yeah," Warwick moaned. "He's a fuckin' con. I never should have ... I should have known he'd back out. He's nothing but a fuckin' *con*. I should have known."

"Sammie's just out raising a little hell," Richard said with a laugh. "He'll come stumbling in around midnight."

"I'm going to bed," Warwick said, his head dropped. "We're leaving early, so get packed. We're gettin' the hell out."

Richard had to feign hunger—his stomach was too tight. He chewed the steak vigorously, but pushed the rest around his plate. She didn't seem to notice, chattering away about the shopping and the late lunch they had on the terrace of the hotel. She could be faking it too, Richard told himself. She's capable of it. She could be playing a role.

"War says Sammie's left," Richard said, folding his napkin. "Where the hell would *he* go?"

"Left?" she asked, her face losing all expression. "Where'd he go?"

"I don't know," Richard shrugged, standing to take the plate to the sink. "He just said Sammie split."

Irene said nothing, her gaze falling to the table. Richard turned and faced her. He waited for her to say something. Perhaps she was waiting for the same.

"I want to take a hot bath," he said.

"That'll be good for your knee," she replied, after a pause.

The water was too hot; it stung and burned without respite. But he didn't care. He knew it was good for the knee. Besides, his whole body was in torment, and the heat worked as a narcotic. He had never been in a tub so large, and he stretched out full length. He closed his eyes, hoping the questions and fears of the day wouldn't pester within.

He heard her enter the bedroom. What a pity the wonderful vacation—the beautiful mountains, the great house, a pretty girl—had been ruined. His life had returned to the agonies of a few days before.

She appeared at the door and said, "War says Sammie's gone back to the States. It's funny he didn't tell me that. I

213

guess he knew it would make War mad. His stuff's all gone. He could at least have said goodbye."

"He found some babe," Richard answered. "And probably didn't like all these fancy people anyway."

"Yeah," he heard her reply.

Surely she's innocent, Richard reasoned with himself. She's not a good liar. Yet how can I know? How can I be sure—and be safe? I don't want to sleep with her, make love to her. How odd. After all these months, she doesn't even seem attractive. With his toe he removed the big stopper.

19

A HEAVY GRAY shroud hung over the valley, as the big Mercedes sped along the curved roadway. They hadn't waited to make breakfast, and Richard's stomach was growling. But his thoughts were occupied by the early morning countryside, with its emerald green hillocks clothed in mist, and the neat, timbered houses draped in sleepy chimney smoke. It was the way east Tennessee would look, if it had the wealth and discipline of the Old World. He turned toward Warwick seated behind the wheel. The face remained creaseless, masking a personality that had to be in turmoil. Richard hoped he was suffering. He deserved more.

"What the hell you staring at?" Warwick growled hoarsely.

"I'm not staring," Richard answered.

"The hell you're not," Warwick barked. "You've been doing it the whole ride."

"What's bothering you?" Richard asked with a sigh. "You've been on edge since last night."

Warwick turned and examined Richard's face. "It's that bum Sammie," he answered. "Nobody walks out on a Morgan."

"Look," Richard chided, "he's probably wandering around with some French gal over in the next valley. We

215

should have left him a note telling him where we're going."

"Shut up," Warwick snapped, "and listen to me. When we get to Zurich I want you to send a telegram to the Parole Board in Jackson, Mississippi. He's supposed to get permission to leave the country, you understand. Don't use any names. Just say he's over here—give the town or something. They'll put a warrant on his hard ass he won't forget. They might even send him back to Fat City."

"Oh, hell, War," Richard argued. "That's a little rough, isn't it?"

"Not for what he's done," Warwick answered, swerving the car to avoid a tractor.

"I don't think Irene would like that," Richard whispered, looking over his shoulder at the sleeping figure.

"Don't say a word," he answered. "What she don't know won't hurt her."

"But what did he do that was so bad?" Richard asked, probing the wound.

"That doesn't matter," Warwick mumbled. "You just do it."

They drove in silence for a while, Warwick squeezing the wheel.

"By the way, where the hell are we going?" Richard asked, stretching and yawning.

"We're gettin' the hell out," Warwick answered quietly.

"Where?" Richard persisted.

"I think Beirut," Warwick answered, making a turn carefully. "Great place. Lots of women."

How different it all sounds, Richard thought to himself. The bravado is all fluff; he's scared and won't admit it. Maybe he always was scared. Maybe the rich are always bluffing behind their millions. But the chips are on the table this time. We're equal. And if he's a coward, he's going to pay for it. He let the silence return, and the lonely, graceful countryside drift past. For once, he leaned back and looked at things which he felt were beautiful and important—even in the face of the challenges to come.

"When are we going to Beirut?" Richard asked casually, lifting a socked foot to the dashboard.

"Sometime tomorrow," Warwick answered distantly.

"There's something I want to do before we leave," Richard said, his head turning to watch a truck gathering milk cans.

"What's that?" Warwick asked.

"I want to get that money," Richard answered.

Warwick paused and then asked, "What money?"

"The money to pay off the trading debts," Richard answered.

"Oh, hell. Why worry about that?" Warwick snorted. "Forget it."

"That's the only reason I came over here," Richard answered, fighting to control his anger. "Otherwise I would have stayed behind."

"Look, the whole goddamn game is over," Warwick

hissed. "Grow up. We've got bigger and better things to look forward to, and you're going to be part of it!"

"I still want the money," Richard said.

"Are you trying to hold me up or something—?"

"Hold *you* up?" Richard growled, before catching himself. "I just want what's mine, and I want it today."

Warwick gripped the wheel more tightly, the color draining from his face. "You're turning on me too," he whispered.

"Bullshit, Morgan," Richard replied. "You're going to live up to the deal."

"Well, are you coming to Beirut?" he demanded.

"I'll decide that later," Richard answered. "I may go back."

"They'll string you up, ol' buddy," Warwick argued, his head swinging from side to side.

"Not once I've got the debt paid off," Richard answered.

"Yeah, but you'll never get a job," Warwick pressed. "You're through back there. They'll fry ya. If you come with me, the world's wide open. I'll cut ya in on all the deals. We'll be a real team, have a lot of fun."

Guilt passed over Richard for a second, until he remembered this was the man who tried to have him murdered. He wasn't going to be taken in again. He was going to get his money.

"I'll always be useful to you back in Memphis," Richard said, after a pause. "You'll need someone there you can trust, and I'll be there. I...won't forget."

The argument seemed to have its effect, Warwick's grip loosening, his face relaxing.

"How big's the debt, ya think?" he asked.

"At least a couple hundred thousand," Richard answered. "You got me pretty big there toward the end."

"We'll settle for two-fifty," Warwick said. "We'll treat the balance as a . . . retainer, you might say."

He's playing every last card, Richard thought to himself. Behind all that facade of generosity is nothing but greed—greed and absolute disregard for anyone else. He needs to be punished, Richard thought to himself, and he will be.

"I just have one condition," Warwick said, after a pause.

"What's that?" Richard asked, preparing for another trick.

"Irene comes with me," he answered quietly. "She gets on the plane with me."

Richard was stunned and withheld his answer for a moment. He hadn't thought about Irene. Ane he knew he didn't have enough time to think through the answer. "Sounds fine to me, War," he heard himself say. "It's only fair."

Richard leaned against the car parked opposite the bank. The wind was strong, blowing leaves and bits of dust and paper in erratic swirls and turns. Spring was in full bloom in Tennessee, he thought to himself. I wouldn't want to live in this climate. He saw Warwick exit the door of the bank and cross the street. He was holding his briefcase in one hand, and an envelope in the other. His glossy hair whipped back and forth in the wind—so different from the serenity of the first time they met.

"Here it is," he said, handing Richard the envelope. "Just remember, I expect the same kind of loyalty I've shown you."

"Absolutely," Richard answered with a smile and handshake. "Absolutely."

"Irene and I are going back to the hotel," he said. "You need to go send that telegram."

The room was almost identical to the one at the other bank. There was nothing to interrupt the bare sameness, except a painting on the wall. It appeared to be a scene from *William Tell*—a man holding a crossbow, his arm placed around a youth's shoulder.

The door opened silently, and a man about his own age stepped inside. Richard remembered the agony of working in such a tightly controlled environment. He wondered what would happen to him if he returned to Tennessee. He could never return to the firm, not after the experiences he had had. But what would he do?

"Your full name, please." The young man asked laconically.

"Richard Harry Johnson."

"Date of birth?"

"March 27, 1948."

"Place of birth?"

"Maryville, Tennessee."

"Can, uh, can you spell Tenn—?"

"T-e-n-n-e-s-s-e-e."

"Occupation?"

"Uh, lawyer."

"I'm a lawyer myself."

"Oh, nice."

"Wife's name?"

"Single."

"Divorced?"

"No."

"Widowed?"

"No."

"Passport number."

"C-66490766."

"Let me have it please, and, uh, bank references?"

"I'd rather not ..."

"That's quite all right. Do you wish to make a deposit?"

"Yes, in cash, if that's all right."

"Why, of course. If you would be so kind as to sign these documents—"

"By the way, do you have a typewriter? I need to type a letter."

"Why, of course; as soon as we're through."

"Thank you very much."

"You're most welcome."

The room had been terribly dry, but steam from the shower made it more comfortable. Richard sat with a towel around his waist searching for an English program on the television. He flipped it off in defeat and considered going to the bar off the lobby for a drink. He turned toward Irene seated cross-legged on the bed, painting her toenails. At any other time in their acquaintance, he would have viewed the simple, clear lines of her body as a form of music—this curve folding gently into that, that shadow conforming and melding gently with another. But now he saw her differently, and it saddened him. He felt an urge to walk to the side of the bed and tell her everything he knew, and then ask her to do the same. He wanted trust and security from her, the very things which had been so important and comforting in the past. But he knew he couldn't. She was now another person. He didn't know where she stood, and he couldn't trust her.

"Where the hell's that damn Sammie?" she mumbled, concentrating on the toenails.

"You want to go down to the disco for a drink?" he asked.

"No," she murmured, straining with the brush. "We're supposed to get up early tomorrow, and I want to make kissie."

Love? How can I do that? Richard asked himself. I don't enjoy love with strangers.

"It's just not like him," she said in her low, soft voice. "He knows it would upset *me*, for one thing."

"Probably found a big card game," Richard replied, turning toward the large glass window and the blackness beyond.

222

"I don't like leaving without hearing from him," she said, plaintively.

"We'll leave word at the desk," he answered, fighting visions of the crack in the glacier.

"There!" she exclaimed, extending her lovely legs under the bed lamp, the paint glistening. "How does that look?"

"Beautiful," he answered.

"Come on over," she said.

For reasons he couldn't fathom, he walked toward the bed. How could he make love to this girl, their lives now so opposed? Yet he wanted relief—a balm—from loneliness and anxiety. She tested the paint with her finger.

"Sure you don't want to dance?" he asked, as she slid between the covers.

"Sure, I want to dance," she laughed, fluffing the pillows.

Her hand then reached his shoulder and began its kneading. It then slid down his ribs and waist toward his buttocks. And he knew that he wanted love, even though confused and distorted. And he leaned farther, to find love with the stranger.

20

THE LAST DAY began abruptly, with the telephone bleating incessantly in the darkened bedroom. Richard pulled himself from a deep sleep and groped through the blackness. He felt a glass slip from the night table, as he reached for the light. The clock showed six-thirty. Who the hell would call at that hour?

"Hello," he said dully, half angry with the intruder.

"It's me," Warwick said, his voice quaking. "Come over—now!"

"What the hell, War," Richard answered.

"Just get the fuck over here!" Warwick pleaded. "Please!"

"Okay," Richard answered sleepily, remembering the letter he had typed and left at the desk. "I hope this is important."

"It is," Warwick answered. "Hurry!"

Richard replaced the receiver and sat on the side of the bed. This was going to be fun, he told himself, yawning widely. Warwick was going to get a little of his own medicine. Besides that, it might even be profitable. He stood up, adjusting the covers around Irene's shoulders. It was probably the last time he would share a bed with her, and he was surprised he felt no emotion. Where did the feelings go? he asked himself. How does such truth evaporate?

He decided not to shower or shave—it was like being on a holiday. He tugged on a pair of jeans and a sports shirt, then slipped into a pair of loafers. He then grabbed the key and tossed it in the air. This is going to be fun, he mused, and I'm going to savor each minute.

"Is that you?" Warwick asked through the door.

"Yeah," Richard answered, rubbing his eyes.

Warwick unlatched the door and opened it warily. He was wearing a silk robe over cotton pajamas. His hair was uncombed, and he hadn't shaved.

"What's up?" Richard chirped, as he strolled inside. "You got any orange juice?"

"Read this," Warwick said, thrusting an envelope into Richard's hand.

Richard carefully opened the envelope and removed the letter. He then read it slowly, line for line. He was rather impressed how well he had captured Sammie's manner of speech—short, concise sentences sprinkled occasionally with poor grammar and typing mistakes. "What the hell's he up to?" he asked, handing the letter to Warwick.

"I told you he hadn't run off for a little fun," Warwick answered anxiously. "He's out to blackmail me."

"But what's the 'file' he's talking about?" Richard asked, falling into one of the easy chairs.

"It's a file I gathered before I left," Warwick whispered. "It...it has everything in it—all the secrets.

If . . . if the . . . wrong people got hold of it, they would not only get everything—but . . . I could go to jail."

"But five hundred thousand dollars—that's ridiculous," Richard snorted, watching Warwick rub his shoulder.

"Maybe," he replied quietly. "Depends on how you look at it."

"But who are the 'friends' he talks about?" Richard asked, standing and peering out the window into the misty dawn.

"That's the Mob," Warwick answered, taking a deep breath of air. "I left owing 'em a little money."

"And the half million takes care of that too?" Richard asked.

"Yep," Warwick answered quietly. "Supposed to."

"I don't see much choice," Richard said quietly. "I sure wouldn't want the whole world . . . gunning for me."

Warwick didn't respond, but continued rubbing himself. He then turned his back to Richard and hunched his shoulders, and they began to shudder. Richard was stunned. Warwick was apparently crying. The one who had been so cruel, so invincible. He watched Warwick much as he had Irene—without emotion.

"You go get the money at the bank," Richard heard himself say. "I'll pack and meet you there. I'll deliver it to Sammie in the park, while you and Irene pack and head to the airport. I'll try to meet you there with the file. Does that sound okay?"

Warwick nodded and then cleared his throat. Without

turning, he said, "I had the money for the Mob in my briefcase, and he took it. How can I trust him now?"

Richard's mouth opened slowly.

Irene had dressed and left for breakfast. Richard hurriedly showered and shaved, agonizing over Warwick's comment. Perhaps Sammie had tried to kill him for his own reasons, and Warwick wasn't involved at all. If that were the case, he was punishing him unduly, and he should end the game. He was confused, but knew he had to pack. One thing was certain—they would all be leaving.

He opened the suitcase and remembered the file. He lifted it from the bottom and slid it into his briefcase. He then remembered the .38 and wondered what to do with it. He couldn't simply toss it into a trash can. Yet where would he put it? He reached into the boot and found nothing. It must have been the other boot. He found the second boot and reached inside—again nothing. He stood in confusion. Perhaps he hadn't put it into the boot—but no, he remembered it clearly. Again he plunged his hand into the boots, and found nothing. He searched the suitcase frantically, finally removing everything. There was no pistol.

Then Warwick must have it, Richard thought, a chill passing over him, and Irene must have helped him. He sat on the edge of the bed, his head turning light. What should he do? If Warwick had the gun, he could figure everything out, and he would be armed and dangerous.

Perhaps he should simply pack and run for the airport. He stood and replaced the clothing.

As he stood at the door, it came to him that they still probably think Sammie is alive and waiting at the park. Warwick wouldn't take the chance; he would hand over the money. He would go to the bank. He would play out the hand.

"It's all in there," Warwick said, handing the package to Richard. "Get the file and bring it to the airport. I can't function without it."

"Don't worry," Richard mumbled, unable to look at his eyes.

The two said nothing for several seconds, an awkward gulf remaining between them. Finally Richard looked up and smiled, and he saw the eyes—big and lustrous and uncommitted. He was moved to say something, to pretend it was business as usual. But he was afraid his voice would betray him, and Warwick had the .38.

Without speaking, Warwick turned and stepped into the taxi. Richard watched him leave and disappear down the Bahnhofstrasse. He knew it would be the last time he would ever see Warwick. He was going to walk to the bank and deposit the money, then rent a car and drive to Germany. To hell with his belongings. He had the money and his passport, and they were all the world cared about. But the occasion gave him pause—after all they had been through. Finally he started to walk down the street to his own bank. It was dangerous carrying so much money on the street, but no one knew. He smiled, as he stopped to take a look at it. A half-million dollars—more than enough to solve all his difficulties. There were some dozen small packets inside. He pried one open with his fingers and saw the tissue paper. It must be the light, he said to himself, resting his briefcase on the hood of a car and opening the package wider. But, no, he wasn't wrong; the packet contained nothing but fine tissue paper. He opened the others quickly, oblivious to the glances of passersby. Again more tissue paper. There was no mistake—Warwick hadn't quit yet. He was going to keep the money and make a break, true to his character.

Richard examined the packets once again, before throwing the whole package into a trash receptacle. At that moment the sun unexpectedly broke through the clouds and flooded the Bahnhofstrasse with brilliance. And the world was transformed—colors otherwise hidden sprang forth, and the faces of pedestrians, otherwise dour, turned cheerful. He leaned his head back and spread his arms and stretched. Perhaps that's the way it should end; perhaps the score was now settled. And he felt at peace with himself, and the world. He would spend a few days enjoying himself, then return to Memphis, to face whatever life offered. He decided to celebrate with a drink. So he lifted his briefcase from the hood of the automobile and walked into a nearby cafe.

The cafe was empty but hospitable. He found a chair near the window and sat down. He leaned back again to stretch and then loosened his tie. To hell with Warwick and all his greed and turmoil, he told himself. He was now free from all that. And he would have a number of days to enjoy it, all by himself.

The waiter brought a glass of cold white wine, and Richard took a long, delicious sip. German wines were so different from the others; they had a softness, almost like a woman's skin.

His thoughts turned to Irene. She too was now in the past. But he wished she weren't; wished that she could be with him to enjoy the coming days. She was surely involved with Warwick, he reminded himself, but she certainly didn't know everything—not about Sammie, at least. She could have simply been a willing victim, like himself. After all, he wasn't completely innocent; he too had wanted the profit, the excitement. Perhaps she was just like himself, wanting the same things. And maybe she would rather spend the next few days traveling with him—willing to face the consequences back home—than fly to Lebanon. He would never know unless he asked her.

Richard stood and placed a five-franc note on the table. He grabbed his briefcase and left the cafe. He walked to the middle of the street, oblivious to the streetcars humming past. A taxi stopped and he stepped inside. "To the airport," he heard himself say. "And please hurry."

Richard stood in front of the sliding glass doors leading into the cavernous departure hall. The hiss and whine of powerful engines wafted through the spring air, bespeaking departure. It was a much bigger building than he had remembered—how was he going to find them? At that moment, he saw Warwick stepping from a taxi at the other end of the walkway. He began running toward them, as he saw Irene appear from the door.

"Hey!" he shouted with a smile. "I thought I was going to miss you."

Warwick looked up in disbelief, a scowl soon covering his face. Irene grinned broadly.

"Listen, you'd better go get your luggage," she said. "The plane leaves in thirty minutes."

"He's not coming!" Warwick snapped, slamming the taxi door.

"I got the file," Richard said, still smiling. "Everything went real smooth."

Warwick paused for a second, then said, "Come over here!"

Richard followed, as Warwick crossed the street and headed toward a parking lot. They proceeded several more minutes, before Richard remembered the pistol. Surely Warwick wouldn't use a weapon in broad daylight, but Richard wasn't going to take any chances. "Where the hell are we going?" he asked. "This is far enough."

Warwick wheeled around, he face contorted with rage. "I thought we agreed you were leaving," he hissed through his teeth.

"Yeah, but you needed the file," Richard answered. "What was I supposed to do, *mail* it to you?"

"Hand it here," Warwick growled, extending his hand.

"Sure," Richard answered, opening his briefcase. "What's the big fuss?"

"Where's Sammie?" Warwick barked, shoving the file into the pocket of his raincoat.

"I left him in the park," Richard answered. "He wasn't too friendly. 'Course I don't think he ever liked me much anyway."

"Now, listen," Warwick hissed, grabbing Richard's lapel.

"I don't like being touched," Richard said firmly, looking at Warwick's hand. "And I want to say goodbye to Irene."

"No!" Warwick shouted, his voice trembling, *"I hate you! Get the hell out of here!"*

Richard stood with his mouth agape, as Warwick struggled to control himself.

"I've always hated you," he finally continued icily, "and everyone like you. You're just a stupid hick—like all the rest. I made you everything you are, but you never figured out the score. The only reason I ever had you around was to *use* you, but you even fucked that up. Now get the hell out of my life, you maggot, or I'll . . . destroy you!"

"I'll have to give Irene some excuse," Richard replied. "I don't want to just walk out on her."

"No!" Warwick shouted, his eyes glaring.

232

"I only want to sit down and have a drink," Richard answered firmly. "The three of us."

Warwick continued his stare, breathing heavily.

"One drink," Richard repeated. "Then I'll leave."

Without reply, Warwick strode past Richard toward the entrance. Richard followed, relieved he hadn't seen the pistol. Warwick walked past Irene without saying a word and entered the sliding glass doors. Richard, Irene, and the porter followed him to the ticket counter. Warwick threw the tickets and passports on the counter, and gazed off into the distance.

"Why aren't you coming?" Irene asked with concern.

"I ... I'm going to stay here to clean up some of the business," Richard answered, so Warwick could hear him. "I'm going to meet you in a couple of days."

Irene's expression collapsed, and she turned her head away. Richard could see her big eyes glisten, and he had the urge to embrace her.

"Let's have that one drink," Warwick snapped, taking the tickets and passports.

They proceeded to their left toward the passport control. Warwick handed Irene her ticket and passport, and they each filed past the guard. They stepped onto the escalator to the waiting room, Richard wondering how he was going to talk with Irene alone. At the inspection barrier, Warwick tossed his two briefcases onto the moving belt. One of them was new, Richard noticed; it must contain the money. Warwick then proceeded through the X-ray gate.

233

Richard and Irene placed their hand luggage on a second belt and passed through another gate. On the other side, the guard held up his hand to Warwick.

"Please open this briefcase," the guard said, resting his hand on the automatic weapon hanging from his belt.

Warwick sighed and opened the snaps to the briefcase. He lifted the top, and Richard heard a collective gasp. He too looked, and there was the glistening .38 on top of the papers.

"No!" he screamed, turning first to Irene, then to Richard.

"Don't touch that pistol!" the guard yelled, fumbling with his walkie-talkie.

And then things became blurred and confused. Richard froze, helpless to act or comprehend—until he heard the enormous *Bamm!*

Screams and shouts ensued, and someone shoved him away. But he kept looking back, back toward the figure sprawled on the floor, his left leg twisted beneath him like a rag doll's, his face disfigured and red and ugly, his hand still grasping the pistol. And there were more and more shouts and screams, as someone kept pushing him farther down the hallway.

"Here!" she whispered urgently. "Take the briefcase. I'll carry yours."

"But where are we going?" he asked.

"I've got tickets," she whispered soothingly. "Hurry, we'll miss our plane."

234

THE WAVES HURLED themselves against the empty beach with fierce irregularity, while the sun, though sinking rapidly, held sway over the helpless blue skies. The two lay still, as if sleeping, she on her back, and he on his side facing her. Without opening her eyes, she spoke.

"You're going back, aren't you?"

"Yeah," he answered, without moving. "Tomorrow, I think."

"What's going to happen?" she asked, sitting up slowly.

"I don't know," he answered. "But it's the only thing to do."

"Will...will you go to...jail?" she asked, staring toward the sun.

"It could happen," he answered, rising to one elbow. "But I think Arnold will help me out."

"We could just stay here," she said. "We have plenty of money."

"That won't work," he groaned, sitting up and grabbing his knees. "It's just not right."

"Can't we at least stay a couple more days?" she cooed, kissing him on a cheek. "It'll still be cold back home."

"It'll be nice in a couple of weeks," he answered.

The two sat mesmerized by the lonesome beauty of the

beach and the incessant emerald waves foaming toward the shore.

"Do...do you want me to come with you?" she asked.

"Why, of course," he answered, looking toward her in amazement.

"I just wanted to know," she said, tears rolling down her reddened cheeks.

"Aw, baby," he responded, cupping her in his arms. "You're all I have left."

"Well, I thought after what Sammie tried to do to you...," she sobbed.

"It wasn't Sammie," he said soothingly. "It was Warwick—we talked about that."

"I guess that I just wanted to hear it," she said, her voice deepening. "I feel so alone."

"You'll never be alone, Irene," he whispered as he kissed her softly. "I'll always love you."

She nodded, and they slowly rose and gathered their things. They then locked arms around waist and began their journey, leaving the sea to continue its restless, endless conflict with the land.